Total-E-Bound Publishing books by Sam Crescent and Natalie Dae:

Forced Assassin
Rude Awakening

SHADES OF GREY

NATALIE DAE and
SAM CRESCENT

Shades of Grey
ISBN # 978-1-78184-514-1

Interior text design by Claire Siemaszkiewicz
Total-E-Bound Publishing

Published in 2012 by Total-E-Bound Publishing, Think Tank, Ruston Way, Lincoln, LN6 7FL, United Kingdom.

Total-E-Bound Publishing is an imprint of Total-E-Ntwined Limited.

SHADES OF GREY

Dedication

It's been great writing with you, Sam!
—Nat

Prologue

In the meeting room of the compound's church, Travis Williams glared at his pack mate, Sam, wishing he'd get off his damn back and step the hell away. Sam stood too close, his eyes blazing, black hair sticking to his forehead with sweat. Any second now they'd get into a fight. Travis didn't want that—he just wanted freedom, the choice to live his life how he wanted, not by some fucked-up pack rules handed down to him because his parents had died. Why should he take control of the wolves just because he'd been born as the son of their leader? What if it wasn't what he damn well wanted?

And it wasn't, Jesus Christ, it wasn't, yet Sam seemed to think it didn't matter, that Travis ought to suck it up and take care of them all like his father had done before him.

Not if Travis could help it.

He was sick of being stuck on the compound, remaining there through fear of being shot and killed. Of people finding out what they were and hunting them down. He'd always had a touch of the free spirit about him, the need to venture away and settle elsewhere.

"It's your job," Sam snarled, drawing closer. "You've always known that, man."

Travis stepped back, his ass butting up against the altar. "Yeah, I've always known that, just like I've always known I didn't want the responsibility when the time came. Fuck, it's like being expected to become a man of the cloth when all you want to do is fuck. It goes against the grain."

"Grain or not, you belong here, leading us." Sam shook his head. "I can't believe you're thinking of running out on us."

"What, you'd prefer me to stick around and lead half-assed, my heart not in it?" Travis sighed out his frustration, shoving away the urge to smack Sam where it hurt.

"No, I expect you to learn how to do it, to rule from your father's instructions. He left you a ledger, for fuck's sake. Everything in it you could need to know. All you have to do is read the damn thing!"

"If it's so easy," Travis snapped, "you fucking take over!"

They stared at each other, Travis on the verge of shifting from anger. He wanted to rip Sam apart, and that wasn't something he'd ever thought he'd want to do. They'd grown up together—were cousins, for Christ's sake.

Sam widened his eyes. "Are you *serious?*"

"Of course I am. I don't want this, never have. You've always been more of a leader. Makes sense that you do it—seeing as you want to…and don't deny it, either."

Sam nodded slowly. "I'll not deny it. I've always envied you, knowing you'd take this position someday."

"So have it." Travis risked a small smile. "It's yours."

"Fuck..." Sam walked away, pacing up and down the short aisle, his footsteps resounding in the echoic church. "You mean it, don't you?"

"Yes!" Travis said, trying not to snap. "I want out of here. I want to live like a normal person."

Sam barked out laughter. "Normal! Hardly..."

"As normal as I can be, then." Travis closed his eyes for a second, imagining packing his bags and getting out on the open road, going wherever the hell he wanted, wherever his instincts took him.

"And what if you're discovered? What then?"

"I'll move on."

"Every time?"

"Every damn time."

Sam stopped pacing, turned to face him, his face grim. "You have the money they left you?"

"Yes. I'll take half, leave the rest for the pack."

"Right." Sam smoothed his hands down his face. "You'll keep in touch?"

"Maybe."

"Maybe? What—you're thinking of a complete break?"

"Yes." Travis felt guilty, but if he didn't walk away completely he'd be persuaded to come back at some point.

"You don't want more time to think about this?" Sam stared at him, pleading silently for Travis to stay.

"No, I'm done thinking." *Just let me go. Let me fucking go...*

"Well, then. I guess this is it, right?"

Relief winged through Travis. "Yep, this is it."

"If you need us—"

"I won't."

By fucking God, I won't.

Chapter One

Travis stood on the edge of Sarah French's ranch and sniffed the air. Shit, he could smell her sexy-as-fuck scent from here, would recognise it anywhere. In his wolf form, despite the night cloaking him, he risked being spotted or shot, but hell…what he'd heard earlier had spurred him into visiting her now.

Seemed local asshole Clark James was intent on making Sarah his woman tonight, regardless of whether she wanted him or not.

That wasn't an option.

Travis narrowed his eyes, cocking his head to listen for hunters. They roamed this area freely all year round, even though they shouldn't be on Sarah's damn property.

A lone woman's requests were easy to ignore.

Bastards.

He looked up at the moon, the big silver ball obscured by thick grey clouds pregnant with rain. He reckoned there'd be a downpour before the hour was up, maybe a storm tagging along for the ride. The autumn weather had been all kinds of crazy lately—

warm one minute, teeming with rain the next. The different aromas the rain threw up messed with his sense of smell, obscuring those he would have caught with no trouble at all in the dryer seasons.

Dangerous.

Deeming it safe, he loped across the grassy field surrounding her white house, keeping his eyes keen to any movement in the shadows. A line of trees stood to his right, their trunks like thick bodies topped with an abundance of hair. The leaves hadn't fallen yet, and in the daytime they were a riot of reds, yellows, browns and oranges. Wouldn't be long and those branches would be laid bare, skeletal arms and fingers stretching into the winter sky.

He'd wanted to make love to Sarah beneath them for the longest time. Since last summer when he'd first rolled into town looking for work. He'd found it, right here on her ranch, and, hell, he'd found the woman of his damn dreams as well.

He reached the picket fence separating her house from the fields and paused. Sniffed again. All he smelt was her.

Good.

He slunk low and crawled under the fence and, on the other side, scoped the area again. You couldn't be too careful around these parts. One wrong turn and you were fucked. Those hunters, Clark James and his cronies, didn't give a shit what they killed. Travis had heard tales of them killing a man once, some hiker kid who had wandered into the mountains at the back of Sarah's place. Denial had come quickly, as though they'd got their stories straight before news had hit the town of a dead body on the banks of Gordon's Creek, but Travis had known better. Had known by the glint in Clark's eyes that something was amiss, had been able to tell by the scent of blood coming off him in waves. Yeah, he might have washed it off, but it had still lingered. A wolf could smell it—no problem.

Baring his teeth, Travis padded towards Sarah's house, heading for the French doors to her living room. He'd keep out of sight, wouldn't want to frighten her, but he had to see if Clark was there. He couldn't smell the man, but Travis wanted to check just the same.

He stared through the glass, seeing Sarah curled up on the blue velour sofa, legs tucked beneath her, a book on her lap. A baby-pink nightgown covered most of her body from his view, and he was glad of that. Wouldn't feel right watching her if she was exposed, unaware he was out here. He was no stalker, no freak.

The fire to the right of her blazed—long licks of yellow and orange flame that pranced frenetically. What he wouldn't give to be in there with her right now. She was beautiful, no doubt about it, the kind of woman every man wanted. Trouble was, most single men around here *did* want her, hanging around the way they did, asking if she needed help with this or that. Apart from Travis and a couple of others, Sarah only employed married men. A sure-fire way of keeping safe, she'd said. He'd asked why she'd taken him on to groom the horses and give them exercise.

"You're different."

And that was all he'd got out of her.

It churned Travis' guts when he thought about one of the other men touching her. Made him see red every time. So why hadn't he told her how he felt? Why did he stand on the sidelines, just being her friend and employee? Simple. Because what woman would believe he could shift into a wolf? What woman in her right mind could accept that? Sarah was level-headed, strong and independent, saw things in black and white. Anything grey didn't figure with her. It was a frustrating trait, one that had led to many heated discussions between them, ending up with him walking away allowing her to believe she was right and he was wrong.

But with Clark fucking James, he wouldn't be swayed. That man was bad to the marrow. Travis would just have to make sure Sarah saw it, that was all.

She shifted in her seat, flicking over a page in her book. He wondered what she was reading this time. Maybe one of those horror novels she enjoyed so much, or a thriller, perhaps. He should have known she wasn't the romance type. No hearts and flowers for this girl. She liked it as real as it could get, true crime being her favourite read, so she'd said.

Her long hair, black as a crow's wing, fell forward, shining from the light of the fire. She tucked the wayward strands behind her ear and brought one hand to her mouth, sucking a thumb tip or biting a nail, he wasn't sure which. He wondered what that hair would feel like running through his fingers, whether the folds of her cunt would be just as soft—or softer. If he wasn't a wolf he'd be hard right now, battling away an erection that threatened to expose how he felt about her. So far, when in her presence, he'd managed to walk away if his cock sprang to life, or to hide it beneath his plaid shirt fronts. Even taking his Stetson off and holding it casually in front—the action looking as natural as breathing, belying the real reason behind it.

A few splatters of rain slapped his pelt, one plopping on the end of his snout. That was all he fucking needed. Yeah, he'd known it was going to rain at some point, but he'd hoped it would be later once he'd seen Clark off. Now the rain would mess with his sense of smell, and if a wind picked up he was in the shit and then some. Frustrated, he growled low in his throat, the hair on his neck standing upright.

Something wasn't right.

He cocked his head again, straining hard, wanting to pick up on whatever had made those neck hairs react. Sniffing did nothing, bringing only a damp-earth stench along with a harder dash of rain. Nothing sounded untoward—no footsteps, no shuffles, no—

Breathing. He heard breathing, all right, and it wasn't his own.

"Well, look what we have here," Clark said, voice smarmy. "A goddamn wolf prowling the property."

Travis spun to face the man, retracting his lips and growling louder.

"You don't scare me none," Clark said, his smile creamy from the light in Sarah's living room. Strands of short dark hair lay flat on his head. "Not when I got me a gun here."

The urge to smack the shit out of Clark gripped Travis, but he couldn't shift, didn't have the time. Besides, if he shifted, the story of him being a wolf would be around the town by dawn, and fighting Clark naked wasn't high on Travis' list.

He stared at Clark, eyeing the small pistol hooked into the man's waistband. If he was quick, he could knock Clark down before he even had time to draw. Decision made, he lunged, all four paws smacking Clark in his shirt-fronted chest. Travis sailed through the air with him before hitting the ground with a dull thud. The rain fell harder, running into Travis' eyes, and he shook his head, blinking to get clearer sight. Beneath him, Clark pushed against Travis' chest with one hand, his other frantically searching for his gun.

Travis wasn't taking any chances. He dipped his head quickly, sinking his teeth into Clark's ear. He wanted to rip that fucker off but held back. All he needed to do was make the man leave, get him off this land until he figured out how best to keep Sarah safe. Her being raped if she declined Clark's offer of being her man just wasn't in the cards, no matter how much Clark had laughed about it earlier. God, that son of a bitch needed taking down a peg or ten.

Travis bit harder, pleased to hear Clark wailing as he smacked at Travis' snout with both hands. Scooting his back end around, Travis sat on Clark's gun and applied a little more pressure to his ear.

"Get the hell off me!" Clark yelled, the sound of the rain drowning out his voice. "You fucking bastard of an animal. Get off!"

Travis released his ear and went for one of his hands instead. He bit, teeth sinking into the flesh. Blood flooded his tongue. Clark's primordial howl almost matched Travis' when he had a mind to cry out at the moon. If this situation wasn't so serious, Travis would have laughed.

"Jesus damn Christ!" Clark said, his breaths heavy pants.

Travis let go and stepped back, snarling and snapping his teeth.

Go, get the hell out of here, asshole. Know when you're beaten.

Cautiously, Clark scooted backwards, only standing when a few feet separated them. "Where's my damn gun?" He looked away for a second to find it—it lay a few metres away—but had a change of heart, returning his sights to Travis.

Yeah, best you fucking forget it.

Clark backed away, clutching his injured hand to his chest. The blood from his ear looked almost as black as his hair in the shadows he'd retreated to, Sarah's living room lights ineffective this far away.

"You goddamned motherfucker!" Clark shouted. "I'll be back for you. I'll remember your hairy ass, you see if I don't."

He turned and ran, boot heels almost kissing his ass every time he lifted them from the ground. Travis watched him go, remaining in place until he was sure the man wasn't coming back. He stood there for a long time, until the moon had shifted some and the rain had gathered speed. Until a giant crack of thunder roared and a streak of lightning fell just short of striking one of the trees.

Turning back to the house, Travis trotted to the French doors and looked inside. Sarah was still reading, oblivious to what had occurred right outside her window. He watched her for a while, mind filled with images of them together, in the past and the future. Memories of her riding the horses, hair swinging, ass raised from the saddle, her thigh muscles prominent beneath her skin-tight jeans. In the future he pictured her much the same way, except he rode beside her and she looked at him in the way a woman looks at a man when she's in love.

Not going to happen.

The sting of something hitting his foot made Travis yelp before he had a chance to stop himself. Pain bloomed, radiating up his leg and burning through his muscles. A shuffle, barely discernible because of the pelting rain and bouts of thunder, alerted him to the fact that, once again, he wasn't alone. He twisted around, grimacing at the ache in his foot, and saw the retreating figure of Clark jumping over the fence and disappearing into the darkness.

How the fuck didn't I hear him?

Too busy entertaining fantasies, that's why, asshole.

He cursed himself a little more, felt the shift start to take over—and panicked. No, no way could he shift. Not now, not here.

Aww, fuck.

Too late. He slumped to the floor, his foot on fire, the rest of his body burning just as bad. The shift seemed to take forever, and, by God, it hurt. It didn't usually, so what was different about tonight? He felt woozy, lightheaded, and, as the final vestiges of his wolf vanished, he looked through the French windows to check on Sarah.

She stood staring at him through the glass, a frown creating deep crevices in her forehead, her mouth open in shock. Had she seen him shift?

Jesus, no. Please, not that…

She wrenched open one door and stood in the frame, hands jammed on her hips and fire in her eyes. "Travis? What in the hell are you doing out here?"

"I…" He couldn't manage much more than that.

"And naked—*naked* in my damn backyard!" She stepped out into the driving rain, walking towards him barefoot. "Of all the people to label a pervert, I'd never have picked you, Travis Williams. Get the hell up and explain yourself!"

He stood, difficult with the pain in his foot, and opened his mouth to speak.

Before he had the chance to form words, Sarah said, "Oh my God. Your foot. It's bleeding!" She knelt, hair plastered to her head now, rain running in rivulets down her face. "Oh, shit. You've been *shot!*"

What?

Travis glanced at his foot. A bloody mess marred the webbing between his big toe and the next.

That fucking Clark…

"Who the hell did this?" she demanded, standing and holding out her hand.

"I don't know." He took her hand and allowed her to lead him into her living room. "The floor. I'm going to get it filthy."

"Fuck the floor!" she snapped. "I'm more interested in your foot."

Normally, he'd have wished she was more interested in his cock, but now wasn't the time for such thoughts. As though knowing he'd been shot had given his body permission to react, the pain grew more intense. It was only a flesh wound, but, shit, it killed like a mad bitch.

She closed the door, snapping the lock into place. "Get yourself into the kitchen. I'll clean you up. And maybe you can explain why you're naked while we're at it."

He lowered his head and walked to the kitchen as best he could, wishing other circumstances had led to her seeing him naked. Still, at least she knew what he looked like unclothed now. The best he could do was let her clean then dress his wound and get the hell home. He'd make up some bullshit about why he was on her property at night and hope he convinced her.

He sat on a pine chair at the table and lifted his foot, balancing it on his knee. Sarah bustled in, draping a blanket around him then going to the cupboard under the sink where she kept her first-aid kit.

"So," she said, dropping it onto the table and taking off the lid. "What the fuck were you doing out there with no clothes on? You got some kind of fetish or something? Enjoy dancing naked in the rain, is that it?"

Travis almost laughed. "No, no, nothing like that. I saw someone walking towards your house with a gun. I'd just got out of the shower…" *There, that should do it.*

"And?" She took his foot in hand and began cleaning it with sterile wipes.

It stung.

"So, I didn't think. I went out to follow and—"

"Got shot your goddamned self. Wonderful."

"That's about the measure of it."

"Well, as you know, I can take care of myself. Thanks for thinking of me and everything, but I really don't need you babysitting me. I've lived here long enough alone since my daddy passed away, and I manage just fine. I have a gun in every room and intend to use them if anyone dares to break inside. So, next time you're naked and you see someone headed here, pick up the phone instead, all right?"

Travis nodded. He hated lying to her, but what could he do? If he told her it had been Clark and she questioned the bastard, he might tell her she'd had a wolf in her yard. It was highly unlikely she'd put two and two together—people around here still didn't believe in shifters—but he didn't want to take the risk.

"Now then," she said, "once I'm done here, I'll make you some tea and get you some clothes. You can take the spare room for the night, if you like, or I'll drive you over the field to your place. Whatever you want."

"Thanks."

"Yes, well, you won't be thanking me in a minute. You really ought to have this stitched or it's going to get infected. So, grit your teeth and hold on for the ride, nude boy."

Chapter Two

Sarah finished dressing his foot, worried in case she'd done it wrong. A bullet wound was completely different from the odd graze or cut, despite the confidence she'd displayed when she told him she'd sew it... That had been a ruse, the protective guard she put in place so no one knew she felt vulnerable at times—not only vulnerable in certain situations, but there was also the fact that this was the closest she'd come to a naked man.

Can a man really be that well built from working on a ranch?

Her mouth watered, and a tightness gripped the pit of her stomach. No man had ever made her feel this way before.

What was it about Travis Williams that made her weak in the knees?

"I really think you should go to the hospital." She gathered her supplies and got up from the floor, trying to keep her eyes averted, but who in their right mind could stop looking at such male perfection? Long, straight black hair that fell to just past his shoulders, a strong, square jawline speckled with stubble that would rasp her cunt if she gave him the chance to get anywhere near her? She licked her lips and hated herself for seeing more of her employee than she wanted to.

Sarah placed the soiled wraps into the bin and her first-aid kit back in the cupboard under the sink.

"Right, tea…tea…" she mumbled, trying to get her head in working order.

Oh, my God! Travis Williams is naked in my house.

She pressed a hand to her heated cheek, then filled the kettle with enough water for two, afterwards pulling cups down from the cupboard, silently chanting what she had to do next. Turning everything into a list helped her to not dwell on the ranch hand—granted, the sexiest and most intriguing of ranch hands—sitting in her kitchen, bandaged and in need of care.

She turned to ask Travis how he liked his tea, jumping when she collided with his chest, the shock causing her to let go of a cup.

In a blur of motion Sarah couldn't be sure she'd seen right, he caught the cup then held it in front of her face.

"Sorry for startling you," he drawled.

The blanket she'd given him was wrapped around his hips sarong style, his chest exposed and close. All she would have to do would be to stick her tongue out to lick a line down that very masculine chest…

Focus, Sarah, focus.

With shaking fingers, she took the cup.

"You know, it's rude to sneak up on people," she accused, turning her back to him.

Instead of taking the hint and moving away to give her some space, he drew nearer. His hands came to rest on the counter to either side of her, trapping her. Why did she like being closed in by his arms and body tonight, when if he'd done this another day she'd have given him hell? Sarah shut her eyes to try to control the pounding pulse in her neck and heart. When that didn't work, she opened them.

Her breath coming in shallow pants, she reached for the tea caddy.

"Do you have one sugar or two?" she asked, trying to pull away from his invading presence.

Was he sniffing her hair?

Sarah put the pot that held the teabags back on the counter with a slam, spun around and pushed at his chest. Travis didn't move an inch, but she gave him another shove and he backed up a step.

"What the hell do you think you're doing?" she demanded, folding her arms under her breasts. The act reminded her how simply dressed she was in her nightie. Her nipples puckered, grazing the cotton fabric. Surely they were responding to the cool night air and not this alarming man standing in front of her—a man who had never alarmed her before tonight. But then he'd never been half naked in her kitchen before, either.

"I'm sorry, Sarah..." He stopped suddenly and looked all around them.

Sarah frowned at his peculiar behaviour.

"I'll be back," he said.

Oh, no.

"I don't think so. Sit down and have some tea," she ordered, pointing a finger at the seat he'd just vacated.

The kettle finished boiling and she placed a teabag in each cup. "Do you take sugar?" she asked.

"What?"

With a sigh of frustration, Sarah asked the question again.

"Two, please."

A few minutes later, she returned to the table with the steaming cups of tea. Travis glanced at them and then looked about again. He seemed on edge.

A wave of thunder echoed round the house.

"They did say it was going to storm. Are you afraid of storms, Travis? Is that why you're behaving strangely?"

He turned his attention back to her, and once again Sarah was struck by his deep, sea-blue eyes. How many times had he looked at her with those piercing blues, which seemed to see inside her down to the very depths of her soul?

"I'm not afraid of anything," Travis said.

Her body responded, her nipples hardening to tight points at his blatant display of masculinity. She took a sip of her tea, trying to bring some normality back to her thoughts. Why, out of all the men available, was it Travis, the latest guy to start working for her, who had her so intrigued?

Sarah hadn't always been known for her sensible actions—she'd had to learn to be the way she was. To fight her own battles and always come out the victor no matter what the odds. After all, she was alone on this huge ranch in the middle of nowhere where God knew what could happen and no one would get to her in time.

She could look after herself and didn't need anybody—especially a man—telling her how to live her life. An invasion of wonderful memories of her father came to mind, and she released a sigh in protest then took another sip of tea. When alive, Daddy wouldn't have allowed anything or anyone to hurt her, no matter what. Even when she'd gone into town, people had treated her with respect. Now, though, it seemed most single men were seeing her as an easy target—a woman who needed a man to run this ranch. Including that disgusting Clark James. That man gave her the creeps with his sneering mouth and perving hands. After only a few minutes in his company, she wanted to run home and take a long, steaming bath to rub his very essence away. In recent weeks he'd become way too familiar. The occasional brush of his body as he passed her in the hallway, even when there was plenty of room. A hand that seemed to have a mind of its own, twirling some of her long black hair.

It was at times like these, being shown a lack of respect from some men, that Sarah really missed her father—the one man who'd shown her the respect she deserved.

He'd been the only man she could stomach for large periods of time—until she'd met Travis.

She glanced up into the eyes of Travis Williams, the man who'd entered her life a year ago and had invaded most of her waking thoughts. He was so different from every other man. He opened doors for her, and argued back at her as if she were an equal. He thought she didn't know when he got hard, thoughtfully removing his Stetson to hide the tightness in his pants. Sarah was a woman, after all, and knew all about desire and lust, even if she'd never been fucked.

Travis placed a hand over hers and gazed into her eyes, the kind of stare where she was sure he could see deep into her soul.

"Where did you go?" he asked.

"Huh?" She hadn't been anywhere.

Lightning streaked and thunder followed, the only noise breaking the silence of the room. They stayed perfectly still for several moments before Travis began talking, rewording the same question.

"You seemed to be elsewhere just a second ago. Wondered where you went."

She shook her head against the fogginess consuming her. She must need an early night. All the hard work of the past few weeks was finally catching up with her.

"I was just thinking about my dad and how it was different around here when he was alive and in charge," she revealed, feeling tears well.

She dropped her head and closed her eyes against the wave of emotion. Her father had always told her crying about something wouldn't solve the problem—it would still be there after the waterworks were finished.

Daddy would still be dead and she didn't have the energy to keep crying over him.

"He sounded like a good man from what I've heard from the folk who knew him," Travis said.

"He really was, strong and powerful. There wasn't anything he couldn't do and he had the respect of everyone." She ran a hand through her hair and stretched, trying to work out the kinks in her muscles from sitting absorbed in her most recent crime novel. Memories of her father always hurt. "It's getting late. Do you want the spare room or would you like me to drive you back over the field to your place?" She really didn't want to go out in this storm any more than she wanted him in her house, but she would rather have him here than drive late at night.

"I'll take the spare room if that's all right with you." He drained his cup then handed it to her.

"Suits me, but I'd better go and get you some clothes. It'll have to be some of my dad's old clothing, as I'm sure you won't want to wear or even try to fit into mine," she joked.

He chuckled and stood as she did.

The gentleman every time.

"Stay here, I'll be back." Sarah left him, moving out of the kitchen and upstairs to the end of the landing. With a deep breath, she opened the door to the main bedroom and was assailed by the smell of a room that had lain dormant and unused.

The furniture was still in the same place and the curtains drawn. After the burial she hadn't been able to bear going through his belongings. It had seemed almost like an invasion of his privacy. She went to the wardrobe in the corner, opening the old wooden door handle. He'd made the wardrobe from scratch, treating the wood and carving it all himself as a wedding gift to her mother. Sarah wondered how long it had been since she'd been in here—she half expected moths or something to come flying out at her.

Nothing. There was just dust, a few layers of it. She'd have to come and clean the mess in the next week. Her father had been a large man, and she knew Travis would fit into his clothes. Travis was a bit taller than her daddy—it would be comical to see his ankles peeking from under the jeans. She took out a shirt and a pair of jeans, closed the door and took one last, lingering look at her dad's room before closing the door.

Mission accomplished, no tears.

Sarah made her way back to the kitchen, shocked to see Travis still in the same place she'd left him.

"You can sit down," she teased, handing him the clothes. "These should fit, but I figure, if you haven't died on me by the morning, I'll drive you over to your place before work starts." She reached out, touching his forehead. "Are you sure you're not getting infected?" she asked, her hand burning from the simple touch. His temperature was high.

Travis took her hand in his and smiled. "I've always had a high temperature, part of the family gene pool."

Sarah couldn't stop the frown forming against his explanation—she wasn't sure anyone could have a temperature that high and still be considered normal. "How does your foot feel?" She may have joked about him dying on her, but she wouldn't like to deal with a dead employee…and, in truth, she wouldn't like to see Travis hurt at all.

"Stop worrying. I've told you I'm fine." He stroked his thumb along her inner palm. "Can I ask you a question?"

"Sure."

"What do you think of Clark James?"

The name alone had her cringing.

"Is that my answer?" he asked, laughing when she pulled the face.

"Let's just say me and Clark James don't dwell all that well. Why do you want to know?" Sarah pulled her hand away from his heat. He was hot all over.

"I just heard something in town about him being…interested in you."

"I don't like him and let's leave it at that. It's getting late and I want to get some sleep before I have to deal with work tomorrow." She moved to the back door and checked the lock, surprised to see her hand shaking. Fucking Clark James. The man was a creep, and she'd heard the rumours all too well. How he was going to visit her and take what he wanted. Did the jerk really think someone wouldn't tell her about his intended abuse? One good thing that had come from her father's legacy was that some people still remained loyal and kept her up to speed about the goings-on in town. As soon as she'd heard that little detail along with a load of other shit, she'd gone and purchased all the guns that were safely within reach in every room.

Sarah French was not a stupid woman, and if Clark James came sniffing around, she would be putting a hole through a part of him—and it wouldn't be anywhere near his foot. Any man—except the man she wanted—would be on the end of one of her handguns.

Fucking losers, all of them.

She flicked the lock then went round to all the windows in the room, making sure they were locked as well. Nothing like protection. If Clark tried to get in, she'd make sure she was on high alert before he even made it into the house.

She wouldn't lie. She liked having Travis with her. She somehow knew Travis would protect her against the other man—even though he was a complete stranger in many ways and she didn't know why she felt the way she did.

Sarah was independent and refused to rely on a man, but she wasn't a fool. For as much as she was prepared and could handle herself, there was no arguing the fact that Clark James was still stronger than her and would be able to overpower her easily. When she gave herself to a man, it would be her decision and no one else would make that decision for her.

Whom she slept with was the final control she had over her life, and she was determined to keep it that way.

Turning the light out, she had Travis follow her as she checked every remaining window and door on the way up. She opened the spare bedroom, which she always kept made up. Her dad had always kept a spare room, and it would seem it was something he'd passed on to her. Not that Sarah had expected any late-night visitors. No one but a few really close friends ever visited her on the ranch.

"I know it's small but it's comfortable. I'm just across the hall, so give me a shout if you feel like death is calling," she told him, checking the windows and looking out at the dark, stormy night. A chill went through her. She massaged her shoulder. Was the storm a sign of terrible things to come?

Her daddy had always said a storm was a sign of change. The last time there had been a storm this bad, her daddy had been admitted into the hospital and he'd come out in a box. This ferocious storm, what did it mean?

Sarah cursed her own wayward imagination and the stories she'd read over the years and smiled, wishing Travis a good night before shutting his door and going to her own room.

She took some time to tidy a little, then went to the window to check the lock. Her breath caught in her throat. She was sure she saw something moving below. She leaned against the pane and looked at the same spot. Was that a wolf? A flash of lightning and the form was gone. Blinking and rubbing her eyes, Sarah closed the curtain and climbed into bed before turning out the light.

She lay staring into the darkness, bringing the blanket more firmly around her. Sleep evaded her for a little while, and it allowed her mind to wander to the man across the hall. Not able to get comfortable she turned over to face the curtain on the other side of the room and watched the lightning, listening to the thunder that followed. Thunder and lightning was a partnership. You couldn't have one without the other. One day she wanted a partnership, to be able to rely on someone the way lightning relied on thunder.

She was way too tired, thinking about relationships with regards to the weather. Sarah rolled over away from the curtain-covered window and gazed at the door. She stared straight ahead, and her thoughts returned to the nude man who'd appeared on her doorstep this evening naked as the day he was born. The quick glimpse she'd got of his cock told her more than his tight jeans how long and thick he was. She allowed herself to wonder what he would feel like pushing his large shaft between her legs. Sarah tried to muffle the sound of her moan in the pillow, closing her eyes as a wave of sexual heat invaded her body. Her pussy grew wet from the image of his cock filling her in the most primal way. He'd be rough and hard. His arms said it all—big and powerful.

With a hand pressed against her damp mound, she closed her eyes, bringing the fantasy to light. In this, the privacy of her own room, she could embrace her wicked thoughts. She moved her hand past her panties, slipped a finger into her wet heat, and stroked her clit as she thought of Travis and his thick cock. She imagined he would take her to the floor to have his way with her, settling between her legs and, without any preliminaries, thrusting all the way into her. She let another moan escape into the pillow then gasped.

With a few strokes along her bud she quietly cried out her climax, the sound muffled only slightly by the pillow.

She came down from her peak slowly, panting as her pussy pulsed with each sensation.

Embarrassed by how quickly she'd come, Sarah blushed. Her eyes began to droop, and her last solid thought before the darkness of sleep claimed her was *I hope he doesn't have great hearing.*

Chapter Three

Travis had barely waited for enough time to pass for Sarah to fall asleep before he crept downstairs. In the kitchen earlier, he could have sworn he'd heard someone outside, even though the thunder raged. Anxious that Clark had returned, he'd been on tenterhooks right up until Sarah had closed her bedroom door. He'd watched her nightly ritual, saw how she checked for security, but a locked door or window couldn't keep a man out if he had a mission in mind.

Especially an asshole like Clark.

He'd found the back door key and, after stripping naked and letting himself out, relocked it so Sarah was safe. Or as safe as she could be while he was prowling the night. He hid the key beneath a heavy rock then shifted, telling himself if she got up and found his pile of clothes he'd say he hadn't wanted to get them wet while double-checking that the man who'd shot him hadn't come back. Whether she believed him or not was another matter—she'd definitely think he had a nude fetish or some other damn quirk—but he'd deal with that if and when the time came.

Determined to find the source of the noises he'd heard, Travis plodded the perimeter of the house, coming full circle when nothing untoward occurred.

Maybe he'd imagined them. They'd sounded like shuffles, perhaps someone walking on the gravelled path out back. He'd glanced out of the window at the time but had seen no one out there. Not that he would have. The lights in the kitchen had made the glass nearly impenetrable—all he'd seen was a reflection of himself standing behind Sarah, pinning her against the kitchen counter. Had he gone too far by doing that? She'd sure spun on him, eyes flashing, and the shove she'd given him had proved she wasn't too pleased at having him so close.

I've got no chance with her. No damn chance at all.

He hadn't been able to help himself, though. The shuffling sound had had him on his feet and behind her within seconds, his need to protect her fierce, and he'd silently thanked God he'd had the excuse to catch that cup. If he'd tried to explain about his speed and suspicions, she might not have believed him. Claiming he had sensitive hearing—so sensitive he could hear despite thunder—was a lame-assed excuse.

But telling her I'm a wolf sounds lamer.

Now, he stared into the night. Rain lashed down, bouncing off the ground then back up again, making it difficult for him to see properly. Damn the weather! He couldn't scent anything other than the stench of wet earth, grass, and his soaking grey pelt. Clark had sneaked up on him before, and who was to say that bastard wouldn't do it again?

Deciding he was better off indoors where he could keep an eye on Sarah, he shifted again—no pain, thank fuck—and retrieved his clothes and the key. He let himself in, careful to secure the door quietly and replace the key where he'd found it. Chilled from the rain on his skin, he grabbed a dishcloth and dried himself as best he could before redressing. He smiled at the thought of Clark outside, looking in to find Travis naked. Would that be enough to warn the son of a bitch off? Him thinking Sarah was Travis' woman?

I fucking doubt it, the pig-headed motherfucker.

Finally warmer, he turned off the lights and moved to the window, standing to the side with his back against the wall. He peered out, squinting to see any discernible movement through the rain. Those trees…they looked hellish freaky from here, what with the clouds having gained a deeper hue, sitting behind them like hulking monsters. He shuddered. Unusual, because normally nothing fazed him. Was it because Sarah was upstairs? Upstairs and vulnerable?

He was wasting his time in more ways than one. Clark wasn't out there, and Sarah didn't want to know Travis in any way other than an employer/employee relationship. It sucked, but, shit, he'd have to get over it. No way would he force his attentions on a woman, no matter how much he wanted her.

With his teeth clenched, fists too, he crept upstairs, wincing as a floorboard on the landing squeaked. He'd hate to wake her. She worked so hard—as hard as any of the men. No one could accuse her of not doing her fair share. Unable to resist, he paused outside her door, keen to seek out the sound of her breathing. It was barely audible but there. The thunder had calmed, a rumble that told him the storm was passing and somewhere off to the west.

Satisfied she was safe, he went into her spare room and sat on the bed. It was a painful reminder of how alone he was. A single bed for a single man. He thought of Sarah in her double, sprawled out on the white sheets, her black hair splayed over the pillows. Shit, he'd give anything to touch it, to draw it across his palm before curling his hand into a fist around it. Something told him she'd be quite the firecracker when aroused, yet at the same time he thought she'd like it soft and gentle, a strong man's arms around her, holding him to her chest. Yeah, she gave off vibes twenty-four-seven that she was some strong broad who could look after herself, but he sensed it was all a façade. Not that she wasn't really strong. No, he knew she was that all right, but there was a part of everyone that made a body crave tender affection, wasn't there?

Sighing, he flung himself backward and tucked his hands behind his head. Stared at the yellowed ceiling in the light of a low-wattage bulb glowing from the small bedside lamp. Thought about the snippets of conversation he'd heard this past year.

When her father was alive, the old man had run the ranch and obviously hadn't had much time or energy for the upkeep of the house. It could do with a lick of paint, and he'd noticed the other day while giving the stud, Sholah, a good workout around the paddock that some roof tiles were on the verge of sliding off. He'd offer to fix the house up for her, but Sarah and her stubborn pride probably wouldn't allow it. He was stuck between a rock and a hard place here, wanting to be more than just the newest man on the block. If he was only her employee, he'd have no trouble asking if she wanted a hand, but with the feelings he had for her raging inside him… No fucking chance.

He closed his eyes, remembering the most recent snippet when he'd stood in line at the mini-mart.

"Tonight. It's gonna be tonight. Can't wait for her no longer. That bitch is gonna suck my cock and suck it good." Clark, that no-good bastard Clark.

Travis had turned to see where the man was, spotting him with Rodney Dukes, another low-life piece of scum, all long, greasy brown hair and unkempt beard. He was a different kettle of fish from Clark, with his neat, short black crop and a face free of beard growth. What the hell those two had in common Travis didn't know. They were eyeing the alcohol, Clark fingering a large bottle of scotch then gripping the neck in his fist.

"I'll have a few swigs of this shit and go visit her place. If she doesn't take me up on the offer of giving me pleasure, I'll just have to take it for myself."

Travis had fumed, wanting to beat the crap out of them right there and then, but had decided against it. Better to face Clark on his own.

And look how that turned out.

Restless and annoyed with himself for losing focus and having Clark shoot at him, Travis got off the bed and paced. If he got any sleep tonight it would be a miracle. He wanted to stay alert because of Clark, but the scents in this house—the aroma of the sleeping Sarah filtering under that damn door—were driving him insane.

He wanted her. Wanted to take her hard and fast then make love to her again, slowly, showing her how a real man should treat a lady, tending to her needs before his own. The seemingly impenetrable wall she'd built around herself wouldn't do her any favours if she was looking for a man. But who said she was? She'd given no indication that she was interested in anyone—anyone at all.

"Fuck!" he whispered, turning to stare at the door.

Before he could stop himself, he opened the door and stood on the threshold, his inner voice telling him to go back into his room but his heart making him step on to the landing. He stood, raking a hand through his hair, lifting the other to his mouth, and he silently rebuked himself. What the fuck was he doing standing out here? What good would it do? Sarah was asleep, and if she wasn't and knew he was out here, she'd more than likely yank the door open and urge him back to bed with the business end of a gun poking him in the chest.

I just want…

He followed his instincts, ignoring the screams inside him to take his hand off the door knob and stop turning the fucking thing. To stop pushing the door open and peering inside, seeing her on the bed just as he'd imagined earlier, illuminated by the soft glow of a lamp on her dresser. Hair spread out, her body covered—all except one leg thrown casually over the covers, delicate toes topped with shell-pink polish.

Jesus fucking Christ.

His cock stirred—the last thing he needed. If she woke and caught him in her doorway with a raging hard-on, he'd be out of her house and a job faster than he could try to explain his intentions. He wasn't here to spy on her or get his rocks off.

He just wanted to see if she was all right.

Then go back to bed. She's fine.

But he didn't want to. Fuck no. He could stand here all night, watching her sleep, taking in the way a light film of moisture sat above her full, bowed top lip.

How the hair at her temples was slightly damp. She was hot, then.

Yeah, she's hot all right.

Fuck it!

He turned, closed the door quietly, and returned to his room. Sat on the bed with his hands dangling between his open legs. Cursed himself a blue streak for falling so hard for a woman he couldn't have. Was that the attraction? Wanting her because she didn't want him? Thinking he could win her over by being the opposite of all the other men, treating her right and refraining from giving her lecherous looks? He'd done that and still had got nowhere. Maybe she thought he just wasn't interested. If she'd have looked a little closer at him after she'd covered him with that blanket in her kitchen, she'd have seen the evidence of how much he wanted her. God, his cock had throbbed…until she'd stuck that needle in his foot and done a bang-up job of closing his wound. All amorous intentions had fled, leaving him with sore gums from gritting his teeth and sweat dribbling down his face.

He glanced at his bandaged toes, knowing when he pushed that foot into his heavy work boot in the morning it would hurt like a bitch with the temper of a demon. His shift earlier hadn't healed the damn thing, and he didn't understand why. Still, work tomorrow he would. No way was he going to give Clark the satisfaction of seeing him limp.

Travis gave in, getting under the covers and closing his eyes. He resisted the urge to palm his cock and jerk off—he wasn't having Sarah think he was a pervert for sullying these clothes. Sleep was a long time coming, but come it did. It claimed him almost without his notice.

* * * *

A sharp scream had Travis sitting upright, his heart pumping wildly.

What the fuck?

It took a second for him to recall where he was and why. Then he was out of the bed and that room, flinging open Sarah's bedroom door. She wasn't there, though her bedclothes were ruffled from where she'd slept. A loud sob came from downstairs, and he streaked along the landing, descending the flight in jumps, anger growing hotter with every leap. Adrenaline ploughed through him, and he ran faster, zipping into the kitchen.

Sarah stood in her nightshirt with a coffee pot in one hand, as though she'd turned from the sink half asleep to find the mess her kitchen had become. Whoever had done this had left the back door open. It swung from the wind blowing in, the net curtains billowing.

It was a clever bastard to have wreaked such havoc without Travis hearing him. What sort of jerk broke in and trashed a room without a sound?

Someone with intent to frighten—he'd bet his last, hard-earned cent on it.

He rushed to Sarah's side, avoiding smashed eggs on the floor, crushing her to him, ignoring her strangled protests and shoves to be set free. A muscle worked in his jaw, and a tic flickered beneath one eye. If he wasn't careful, he'd shift. Fuck if he could risk that now. Taking a deep breath to calm himself, he stroked her hair, hating the fact that he could only be doing so now in circumstances he'd rather not entertain.

"Stay there," he said, stalking over to the back door and closing it. He stared out at the grounds, grey in the just-dawn light, and saw nothing that could raise his hackles. Locking up as best he could with broken bolts, he strode out of the kitchen, searching the living room and coming up empty.

"Follow me," he called, waiting for her to join him in the hallway. "I need to check upstairs, but I don't want to leave you down here alone. When we get up there, go in your room and lock the door."

She nodded, still holding that damn coffee pot, her eyes wide, great pools of fright before she composed herself, shutting weakness out and replacing it with her usual mettle. Those eyes went blank then, slates of hardness, and his heart went out to her. He wanted to hold her again, let her know everything would be all right—but not until he'd made sure this house was safe.

He jerked his head towards the stairs, and she followed him up, waiting on the landing while he checked her room. Giving it the all-clear, he allowed her to go inside, and she stepped in, closing the door. He waited for the lock to meet its keeper then inspected the other rooms, finding nothing but furniture shapes in the shadowy gloom.

Anger doubled inside him as he leaned against the wall beside her door. He knew who'd broken in. Knew why Clark had done it, too. The bastard thought Sarah would turn to him for protection.

Christ, I hope she doesn't.

He knocked on her door. "It's safe, Sarah. Come on out."

She unlocked then opened her door. She'd tied her hair into a loose knot, her obviously rushed moves ensuring stray tendrils of black hung down around her face.

Damn, but she was beautiful.

"I'll take you home now," she said, shoving past him and taking the stairs.

"What? Just like that?" He followed. "You have a break-in, and you expect me to just go home and leave you here?"

"I can take care of myself," she snapped, rounding the newel post and striding into the kitchen.

He jogged to keep up. "No. No fucking way! You're not staying here alone after this."

She spun to face him, eyes flashing. "Who the hell says I'm not?"

"Me!" he said, clenching his hands.

She glanced down at them. "And you doing that is supposed to make me feel safe, is that it?"

He unclenched then held his hands up in surrender. "I'm angry, all right? Nothing to be afraid of. I wouldn't hurt you."

She turned away and walked to the fridge, curling her fingers around the handle, then froze. She stared at the fridge door.

"What? What's wrong?" Travis took two strides and he was beside her. He stared at a note, held to the door with electrician's tape. "What the fuck?"

You're mine.

"Oh, you've got to be fucking kidding me," Travis said. "Of all the things a guy could say, he chose that?"

He snatched the note and looked at Sarah. She'd paled, but steely resolution filled her eyes.

"I know who this is," she said.

"So do I."

"I can deal with him."

"No, you fucking can't."

"*Yes,* I fucking *can!* Don't tell me what I can and can't do, Travis Williams. He's been a creep for months. I just need to tell him I'm not interested and he'll back off. Tell him that if he doesn't he's out of a damn job."

Travis let out a snort. "Oh, come *on,* Sarah! You think doing that will stop a man who thinks nothing of getting inside your home and wrecking it? Leaving sick notes? He'll keep on until he gets what he wants, you must see that."

"Whatever!" She waved a hand as though dismissing him.

It danced on his last nerve. "Why the hell can't you see anything other than black and white?"

"Why the hell do you have to see every colour under the fucking sun?"

She glared at him, cheeks flushed, and Travis glared right back, refusing to be the first one to look away. It took more than a minute before Sarah's gaze faltered, and she spun away, growling in frustration, her hands bunched. She walked to the sink and stared out of the window, knuckles white from her grip on the ledge.

"I left the coffee pot upstairs," she mumbled.

Travis walked up behind her, mindful not to touch. "Forget the fucking pot. When you approach him, Sarah, I want to be with you."

"No. No, I can do this on my own."

He wasn't going to be able to talk her out of it, he knew that, and short of following her around all day, he risked Clark catching her alone.

Fuck!

"Well," he said, keeping his voice low. "Just know that if I hear news of that motherfucker touching you, I'll rip his throat out."

Chapter Four

Who the fuck did this man think he was?

So, yeah…she was scared. Someone had come into her domain and ruined the kitchen, but that did not give Travis the right to order her about like that.

Clark James needed a kick in the bollocks and a few choice words, which she was so going to give him when she went to the local bar tonight. If Clark wanted to cause her shit then she would be more than happy to reciprocate. Under no circumstances was she having a man tell her what to do, and Clark James would be the last man to do it.

Sarah couldn't deny how much she'd like to see Travis put those muscles to good use in ripping Clark's throat out, but then she wouldn't see him again because of the whole getting-caught-murder-sentence thing. Not many people had a bad thing to say about Clark—she didn't know why but the whole town seemed to think he was great—or, if they did dislike him, they kept on the tough man's good side. He did, after all, have his cronies surrounding him at every turn.

"Arguing like this will get us nowhere," she said. "Now—it's clear Clark isn't here, so I'm going to go and get my coffee pot, otherwise nothing will be happening but me scratching your eyes out, got it?" She pushed past him, making her way upstairs.

He shot his hand through the slats of the open banister and grabbed her foot.

"Do you mind?" she growled.

"You keep yourself safe, understood?"

If looks could kill, Travis Williams would be flat on the floor.

"Get your hand off me," she ordered, leaning over the banister to glare at him.

For several seconds he didn't move, and anger curled inside her, ready to explode. Sarah wasn't about to admit how much she liked him touching her. It was all too much. She'd had a shot man on her door step, sexual frustration alongside her home being violated, Travis' domineering presence and Clark throwing his threats around. She was ready to swipe at the first person to walk past.

Didn't anyone respect a woman's kitchen anymore? The one domain she'd even refused her father when he was alive was all hers. No one else had the right.

He removed his hand from her foot, freeing her to move on.

"Thank you," she ground out before running up the stairs and slamming her bedroom door.

Her anger was short-lived. Her house wouldn't last long if she gave in to all of her frustrations. She checked her door to make sure it wasn't damaged. Another idiot-proof carpentry book would have to be purchased if it was. The house was practically falling apart, and there was no spare cash to bring in a plumber, builders, electricians, and environmental specialists. She was sure her house would annoy those green people who were shouting out about global warming and whatnot, but, unless she remortgaged, it'd have to stay as it was.

Did she even have insulation?

Sarah decided the door would last a little longer and changed into her jeans—she would need some new ones soon as they were loose—followed by a simple, plain black T-shirt. After making the bed, she picked up her washing and the coffee pot—having to restrain herself from drinking its cold contents—then made her way downstairs in time to see Travis had cleaned up the eggs and was now picking things up and tidying her kitchen.

Sarah saw red.

"Don't touch a fucking thing." With the coffee pot in hand, she stormed over to him, taking the broom out of his hands.

"I'm trying to help," he explained.

"I don't need your help at all." Fuming, she stormed over to the worktop, put the pot in its place on the machine, and set it to reheat the dark liquid. "Do me a favour and go and do something outside. Check the horses or whatever it is you do." She shook one hand at him, then swept up the bits of broken china and bent cutlery that were repairable, placing each item on the table.

The door closed, letting her know he'd finally done as he was told. This would teach her to have sexual fantasies at night about a man she could never have. After today she would become a nun. Sell this ranch and say 'fuck you' to everyone and go join a convent. Between her father and the men in town and now Travis all treating her as though she was a simpering woman who couldn't cope by herself, she was ready to call it quits.

After half an hour or so, she had all the pots and other undamaged stuff on the table and was finishing the sweep-up of the kitchen floor. Years of toiling with her father had made her fast when at work, and she also couldn't stand a mess for long.

By the time Travis made it back to the house, Sarah was sitting at the table on her third cup of coffee. She couldn't believe her luck. That Clark jerk hadn't wiped out her entire refrigerator when he'd strewn food about. She may need her coffee, but she loved full-fat milk in with it, and if he'd emptied the milk cartons there would have been more hell to pay.

Travis came through the door with another man following him. Sheriff Stephen Laurie entered her now-spotless kitchen. The older man was taller than her but not as tall as Travis, with blond hair and a boy-next-door look to him. Kind blue eyes completed the picture and showed why everyone loved Stephen. He wasn't filled out by muscles like Travis, but he could hold his own in a fight.

"Morning, Stephen." She couldn't help but show her annoyance at Travis for bringing the other man here and frowned at him—hard.

"Hiya, Sarah. Travis here said you'd been broken into last night but you didn't hear anything." Stephen glanced around him, obviously looking for the damage.

Sarah got up from her seat and offered Stephen a coffee. She'd gone to school with the man's younger sister and so she'd always had a bit of a soft spot for him—even if his sister no longer spoke to her.

"As you can see, nothing that a bit of elbow grease and hard work couldn't fix. Some dishes broken, a few eggs smashed on the floor, but they can be replaced." She was prepared to handle this problem herself. No one but her was going to show Clark a thing or two.

Travis had gone to the sheriff's department without her permission while she'd been cleaning. How had he got there so fast anyway?

"Could I have sugar?" Stephen asked.

Smiling, Sarah handed him a coffee with sugar and slammed another cup of black into Travis' chest, not caring if the liquid spilt over him. The cheeky shit could live with a little hot water.

"Sorry, Stephen. Travis brought you out here for no reason. I'm sure he'll compensate you with the cost of gas." She turned to the man in question and shot him a beaming smile.

He ignored her, took a sip of his coffee, then began talking to Stephen. "I'm sure Sarah would like to tell you who broke in?"

"Do you know who would do this to you, Sarah?" Stephen asked.

She cursed every man living, got up, went to her fridge and took out some eggs that had survived the break-in. "I know who did it, and I'm not saying who it is, so you can leave my house as I won't be pressing any charges. I'll handle this the good old French way."

She put the eggs on the counter near her cooker, got a bowl and started cracking them into it. She found it soothed her, pressing the egg on the side and splitting it open, letting the contents drop inside. It made her think of Clark's head doing the same thing.

"Sarah, you need to be sensible—"

She didn't give Stephen time to finish his sentence. Whirling round, she pointed her finger at both men in turn.

"I may be a woman but I know how to handle myself. Now, unless you want me to go and get my pistol, I suggest, Stephen—you go back to work where people need you…and Travis—get out of my house!" She went back to her eggs. She was hungry today so she'd have four. Who cared about diets, calories and cholesterol anyway?

The door shut behind the two men, and she didn't catch any of their conversation.

Fucking idiot men.

She whisked the eggs until they formed a golden yellow gloop. Pulling a pan off a wall hook, she placed it on the high heat and melted the butter before pouring in her well-whisked mixture. She didn't like them when they were runny puke and guessed that chefs would call her version overcooked with the texture of rubber. She retrieved a wooden spoon and began cooking.

What could she do to make Clark leave her alone? It was Friday, so tonight would be the best time to warn him away from her—in public so she had witnesses. It would probably help that Stephen now knew Travis had stayed with her. The town would really be rife with gossip and speculation about her situation once the sheriff opened his mouth. All the nosy bastards wanting to know her business. Again she wondered if it would be easier to just sell and leave this shithole.

Several minutes later, she plated up her scrambled eggs and was eating them with bread and butter when Travis returned. She had her back to the door but would recognise his footsteps and scent anywhere.

"Thought I told you to get out of my house," she said, not bothering to turn around, her awareness of him so acute it was frightening.

Travis was different, and it was like her body knew him. Whenever he was in a room her body came to life, even in a crowded one. What was so special about this man with the intense blue eyes?

Instead of answering her or walking out the door, he came and sat in front of her, using his big blues to all their worth.

Sarah lifted her cup and drank in an attempt to avoid eye contact.

He covered her hand with his as she laid it on the table, still holding her fork.

"Sarah, look at me."

He sounded so earnest she was immediately drawn to him. Her heart ached to hear the concern in his voice. She'd do anything to take the worry away, yet she'd been behaving like a brat. Who would blame him if he didn't want to stick around? She gave him mixed signals all the damn time. She licked her lips and watched his gaze drop to the simple movement.

"I'm looking at you, Travis," she whispered. His name rolled off her tongue like smooth butter.

Her throat went dry. He moved his hand to touch her face, his fingers running over her skin. She held her breath, not wanting to ruin the moment she'd created.

"I couldn't live with myself if anything happened to you," he said, his sincerity cutting her to the core.

No one, besides her father, had ever cared about her. She had no friends—none to speak of these days, anyway. So much for keeping the spare room made up for visitors. The women in town thought she was competition for the attention of their husbands. Not that she would ever be a home-wrecker, and there was also the moral dilemma of sleeping with a married man. She didn't have the inclination to make her life so difficult, with the sneaking around and lying to people.

It suddenly hit her how alone she was in this world. Her mother had died in childbirth with the son her father had craved more than anything else in his life. Her sex had been the one thing she couldn't change, and she'd lain awake many nights as a child, praying to be a boy.

Tears welled as the turmoil of the last twenty-plus years consumed her.

"Don't cry, baby." Travis went to the floor at her knees. He took her face between his hands and brushed the teardrops away.

She hadn't cried in so long, she wasn't sure she knew how to anymore.

And he'd called her baby. A slip of the tongue? Just a friendly endearment? God, she hoped he'd meant it in another way, a special name just for her, but she'd never get that lucky.

"Please don't pity me," she sobbed. The tears wouldn't stop falling. She thought of her father and the reprimand he used to give for her crocodile tears, the laughter of the kids who used to tease her at school for her boyish ways.

The pain, the raw emotion, was uncontrollable as tears spilled down her cheeks and onto his hands.

"I'm...so...sorry..." She hiccupped between each word.

"You're in shock, honey, from what's happened. Let it all out."

Travis took her in his arms and Sarah didn't pull away. For once, she wanted to be hugged. She turned into his chest and released all the pain, heartache and nightmares, safe and secure in his arms as he took care of her—the first man who'd taken care of her in so long. She would always love her father but couldn't deny he'd kept her at a distance, and once she'd become a teenager, hugs and kisses had been off the affection menu.

When was the last time a person had given her attention without sexual expectation attached to the comfort? Being held and cosseted was something she'd come to crave since her father died yet she'd been too proud to ask for it.

"Let it out," he chanted in her ear.

And, for the first time, Sarah just allowed herself to be cared for, to give in to releasing years' worth of repressed tears.

She would deal with the crazy later.

* * * *

The only problem with tears, they left a person with a huge headache and a sore throat, along with a face that felt rough and raw. Sarah awoke upstairs in her bedroom, frowned against the late morning light, and checked the time on the bedside clock. She groaned and sat up, testing out her rested muscles.

Jell-O could be the only way to describe her protesting body.

She opened her door and listened to see if anyone was in her home. Silence met her. With a shake of her head, she went to the bathroom to brush her teeth and freshen up her face. The mirror above the bathroom sink revealed the damage unleashing her emotions had created.

"Why couldn't I just keep it all in?"

Now she would have to face Travis with the knowledge that he'd held her as she'd cracked under the pressure.

That was her worst fear—not being good enough or as good as her father…or the son he had so wanted had the child been born. The men who worked for her deserved a leader like her father, who was much better than her.

"That's enough pity party, Sarah French. This is your life and you love it."

Her reflection stared back, not giving her any answers.

Turning out the light—and surprised the damn thing didn't blow up with the way her luck was at the moment—she went downstairs and found Travis, complete with toolkit and screwdriver, working on her door.

She tucked wayward strands of her hair behind her ears and watched him work. God, his muscles stood out beneath his T-shirt, and his suntanned biceps rippled with every movement he made. She wanted to run to him, to smooth her hands over his exposed skin and bury her face in his chest. To breathe in his scent and allow him, just for a minute, to make every bad thing disappear. A second after she thought it, she batted the prospect away, allowing her strong will to overpower any weaker emotions.

"Did you sleep well?" he asked.

Not used to being questioned about her well-being, Sarah stared at him. Why would he ask? Why did he even care?

He stopped working and came over to her, ran his hand through her hair and kissed her on the lips. A quick brush, but it was still a kiss. His closeness thrilled her, and that kiss! The feel of his mouth on hers lingered as though his lips were still there. She dashed out her tongue in an effort to taste him, but he hadn't left anything behind except the tingle of his touch. Her knees weakened, and his breath, hot on her face, almost had her sinking into a chair.

"Did you sleep well?" he repeated.

Sarah frowned and touched her lips.

Travis just kissed me?

The urge to run a finger over her lips was intense but she fought the battle.

"Yes, I did, thank you." She wasn't sure what to do at that moment and nodded in a jerky motion.

"Take a seat and I'll pour you a coffee." He pulled out a chair for her.

"Thank you."

Sarah sat and couldn't take her gaze away from him as he busied himself in her kitchen. She admired his fine ass and noticed he didn't walk with a limp. A man who'd been shot in the foot the previous night would start to feel the injury of a bullet wound after being on their feet all day, wouldn't they?

Travis brought her a cup of coffee with milk—exactly how she liked it—and she glanced at his foot, covered by a work boot.

Wouldn't that hurt like a son of a bitch?

Curiosity getting the better of her, she returned her attention to his face.

"How's your foot?" she asked.

"What?"

"How's your foot? You got shot last night, remember? And I noticed you didn't tell Stephen about *that*."

He moved away from her. "My foot's fine."

He continued his work on the door in silence, but Sarah wasn't fooled. Last night she'd applied her limited skills to his foot, and she knew he should at least be feeling sore, if not a constant burn.

She sighed and let it go, knowing she wouldn't get a straight answer from him. She'd let him fix her door—she didn't know how to so she might as well sit back and enjoy the show.

"There's a lot of work that needs doing around here," he finally said, gesturing to the whole house.

Sarah snorted.

"You noticed that?" She couldn't help but laugh. A lot of work was an understatement. She wondered if it would be easier to demolish the house and start from scratch—that might be quicker to fix. Not the cost, though. To rebuild this beauty from scratch would be a nightmare.

"It's an old house?" he asked.

"Several generations on my dad's side, or so he told me."

"Makes sense. A house like this needs a lot of love, time and attention."

"Along with a lot of money, and the last time I checked notes weren't growing on trees," she snapped.

Why did she speak to him like that? One minute she wanted him to care for her, and the next she fought for control. She ought to watch her damn self. She'd chase him away if she wasn't careful. It wasn't Travis who pissed her off. The constant pain in her ass were the repairs needed to bring this place up to its original glory.

"Have you had quotes off people?" He shut the door and then opened and shut it again.

"What are you doing?" she asked, agitated by her spiralling emotions.

"Testing the door. No squeak, and it's opening and closing with no problems. I just need to fix these bolts into place and the job's done." He pulled out a couple of new bolts and began to open the packets.

"You don't need to do that." She got to her feet to test the door. "How much do I owe you?"

"Yes, I do need to do this, and you owe me nothing." He visually measured a large bolt against the door.

Sarah wanted to refuse the help but knew it would be useless. "Show me?"

"Sorry?"

"If I can't pay you and you won't stop, then please show me what you're doing so I know how to do it next time." Not the best way to spend her Friday afternoon, but it was better than going stir-crazy thinking about confronting Clark James tonight.

"How about you make me dinner and we'll call it even? I can do these repairs no problem, and as payment you can feed me sometime," he suggested.

"No. Show me and I can still do everything else."

"This is not something I want you doing," he warned.

Sarah spread her arms wide. "Look around you, big guy. Who else do you think the upkeep falls to? Me, that's who, and I'm not having anyone else telling me what I can and cannot do. My house, my repairs, my rules. Now show me," she ordered.

He charged towards her, blocking her against the wall with his body. "Not a chance. I'm doing these repairs and I refuse to sit back and watch a woman fix her house with no man waiting for you in case you fall."

"What the fuck is that supposed to mean?"

"Watch your language. Swearing doesn't become you."

Fire burned in her belly, smouldering with his instructions and reprimands, but she didn't want to get into a fight with him.

"Please, just show me the repairs. I have a place to be tonight."

The moment the words sunk in, he tensed. "What did you just say?"

"I've got a place to be tonight."

"You're so not talking about going after Clark James on your own, are you?"

"What if I am?"

Bad move, Sarah, very bad move.

Chapter Five

"What if you are?" Travis stared at her, wondering just how far her pig-headedness would go. She was serious, he could see that all right, but holy fuck, he couldn't let her do it. "If you try and tackle him alone…" He shoved a hand through his hair. "Sarah, that man… I heard him in the mini-mart yesterday. He was with that asshole Rodney Dukes."

She stared at him as if to say, '*So what?*'

Should he tell her? Let her know exactly what Clark had in mind? Fuck it. She had a right to know. The break-in had made this a whole lot more serious, and if she wasn't going to let him hang around her place after work hours, he'd have to shift and patrol the grounds every night. With his sense of smell fucked up for whatever reason and his hearing less than stellar, he might not be much good even then. Add on to that a lack of sleep, and she'd be in danger anyway.

"He said if you didn't want his attentions he was going to force them on you."

"What?"

"You heard me. Stop doing that shit."

"What shit?" She rammed her hands on her hips.

Crap, she had that look about her—eyes ablaze, mouth in a tight line, a deep frown growing deeper—that told him she'd mastered going from soft to stubborn in an instant. She was up one minute and down the next, prickly as hell, too. He didn't need another sparring match with her—God knew they'd had too many to count since he'd started working here—but he couldn't let this rest.

"Making out like you don't know what I'm talking about. *That* shit." He sighed and decided on a calmer approach. "Listen, honey." Damn, he'd called her baby and honey earlier and honey again just now. He had to get his brain into gear before he let his mouth give him away. A woman who wasn't interested didn't want to hear that crap. "Clark's a time bomb waiting to go off. He wants you, isn't going to rest until he has you, and I'm fucked if I can allow him to push into your life like this. You saw what he did in here." He gestured around the kitchen.

"We don't even know it was him." She cocked her head a little and studied him hard, eyes narrowed.

"Oh, come on! Don't give me that bullshit, woman!"

So much for the calmer approach.

She widened her eyes, looking at him as though he'd seriously overstepped the mark, and perhaps he had, her being his boss and all. But this was more than just a boss/employee situation. This was a man protecting a woman. Fuck, he couldn't let her go off on a mad mission to have words with Clark. That bastard wouldn't think twice in showing her up in front of his cronies...although if women were present Sarah might be treated to the nicer side of the man. He was the type to keep his options open, and once he'd had Sarah, he'd move on to the next pretty face and hour-glass figure. No, Clark wouldn't allow his future lays to see the nasty side of him.

"Where were you planning on going?" he asked, voice even.

She moved as though to turn away, so he grabbed her wrist and spun her around to face him, pressing her back against the wall. She winced at his tight hold and, disgusted with himself for exhibiting force, he loosened his fingers. She'd think him a bully if he didn't watch himself.

"I'm sorry," he said. "I didn't mean to hurt you. Please, if I let you go, will you just hear me out?"

"So long as you take a damn step back and give me breathing space." She glared up at him, hair almost free from the knot she'd tied it in this morning. "I haven't got any work done today either, so you need to be quick. I napped, remember? The men are going about their business, but I wanted to sort out the purchase of a new mare for Sholah to get used to. That idea's out the window until Monday now. Shit!"

"Are you deliberately changing the subject? Trying to take my mind off what we were discussing?" He still hadn't let go of her wrist—wouldn't until he was sure she wasn't going to bolt through that doorway to chat with one of her workers as an excuse not to continue their conversation.

"Are you deliberately accusing me of doing that so I get angrier and you can do what you usually do and tell me I'm proving just how hotheaded I am, which then leads to you being able to say that's exactly why I can't do what I want to do?"

She had an answer for everything, he'd give her that. Christ, her mind was sharp. "No. Listen, please, we have to talk this through. Will you just give me a minute?" She didn't answer, so he pressed on, keeping his tone low and soft. "If you're thinking of going to Macy Jo's bar, then maybe you ought to let me come with you. Clark goes there on a Friday to get rat-assed, you know that. Rodney Dukes will be there, as well as all his other freaky friends. None of them will stand in Clark's way if he turns on you. He broke in here without making a sound—neither of us heard, anyway—so, if he's stealthy enough to do that, think what he'll do if you piss him off with your accusing finger and threatening tongue!"

Sarah stiffened, staring at him as if she teetered on the brink of giving in.

Please let her see sense. Just once…

"Macy won't let him hurt me." She lifted her chin defiantly.

"But what if Macy steps out a while? What if John Baines is the only one behind the bar? That guy is almost as bad as Clark with his wild ways at times. I worry about you, Sarah. I don't want you getting hurt."

She huffed out a blast of air. "You only worry because if something happens to me you'll be short on wages."

Ouch.

"What the hell's gotten into you? You really think so little of me as to believe that? I don't give a shit about the wages! I give a shit about *you!*"

Fuck. Aww, fuck.

She gawped at him, blinking rapidly, high colour staining her cheeks. "No, no you don't." She backed away, unable to get far with his grip on her wrist. "Let me go. I must see to the men."

"Sarah?"

"What?" She gritted her teeth.

"Didn't you hear what I just said?"

"Of course I did, I'm not deaf!"

"So me telling you I care about you means nothing?"

He didn't want an affirmative answer, but, hell, he had to know one way or another. If she said his affection meant jack shit, he'd pack his bags and get the hell out of town. Staying here when she didn't want him would hurt too much. He could start again—he'd done it countless times before when people started getting too close to finding out what he was—but he was fucked if he'd ever forget her.

"It means nothing," she whispered. "Now let go of my goddamn wrist and move the hell away!"

He'd sworn he'd never push himself on a woman, but instead of letting her go he pulled her to him, holding her clamped to his chest. Leaning down, he pressed his mouth to hers, sliding his tongue along the seam of her lips, praying she'd open up for him. If she didn't, then he'd have a firmer answer than that she didn't want him.

She closed her eyes and parted her lips, flicking her tongue out to invite his inside. Fierce longing overtook him, and he held her closer, tighter, showing her the best way he knew how that she meant more to him than being just his boss. A low whimper left her, reverberating on his tongue, and he took it as a sign she was eager for more. Braver now that she'd melted a little, he closed his eyes and trailed one hand up her back, caressing the swell of her ass cheek with the other. Fuck, but she felt good, moulded to him the way she was, as though she'd been made just for him.

She raised her hands between them, smoothing her palms up his chest and over his nipples. Sensation rocketed through him, goosebumps spreading right along with it. Excitement pooled in his belly, transferring from there to the root of his cock. He moaned, holding her tighter still, fingertips digging into the soft flesh of her ass. His cock twitched, growing so damn fast he almost lost his breath. He canted his hips, gently pushing into her lower belly so she could feel his need.

Sarah broke their kiss, gazing up at him, all anger erased from her eyes. He felt for her, for whatever reasoning she had going on in that pretty little head of hers that forced her to rebuff help from any man. But, hell, if she pulled away now…

"I don't want you to care for me," she whispered.

"Why the hell not?" He swallowed, throat tight. "What's so bad in letting me help you every now and then?"

"Every now and then. That's why. I can't just have you every now and then, and that's all it would be, isn't it?"

"Why would you think that?" Had someone in her past loved and left her? Used her? He didn't know—didn't know much about her because she gave very little away. When she'd cried earlier, let out whatever emotions she'd been holding in, he'd thought he'd made some headway. Her icy veneer had turned to water—it had washed away whatever sorrows made her seem so cold and angry most of the time, only for them to return now—mistrust the main culprit if her words were anything to go by.

"Because you're a man," she said.

"I don't understand." He frowned. What bastard had upset her apart from Clark? If he got his hands on them… The hairs on the back of his neck stood on end. Fuck, he didn't need that now. He willed himself not to shift, to remain a man so he wouldn't scare her shitless, make her even more wary.

"Men don't want bossy women like me. They want someone they can control. Who'll do as they're told."

He threw his head back and laughed then, loud and hearty. The danger of him shifting disappeared. "You think I don't know I can't control you? Shit, the arguments we've had would tell anyone you're a stubborn woman who wants things all her own way."

"You really think that?" She furrowed her brow.

"Well, don't you?"

She nipped her bottom lip with her teeth, thinking, he'd bet, and he took the time to caress her some more, softly, with no rush. She felt fine, so damn fine, and she didn't move away, didn't look uncomfortable from what he was doing. That was something, wasn't it? A start?

"Is that how I come across?" she asked, running a fingertip around the neck of his T-shirt.

Her skin met the dip below his Adam's apple for a second, and he held his breath. Fuck, his cock and bollocks ached. He could taste her on his tongue and wanted another sample, but kissing her now wouldn't wipe the creases from her forehead and the hurt from her eyes.

"Kind of." He rushed on. "But it isn't a bad thing to want your independence, and I understand it must be hard allowing other people to help you out when you've been used to doing it all yourself. The men working for you—that's different, I get that. But a man around the house? Yeah, I can see why that would get your back up. But I'm here for you. I'll help you out when the work day is done."

"I can't—"

"You can, honey. It doesn't make you weak. Think of it as delegating. You're the boss. You can ask the men for help by way of giving orders if it makes you feel better. Anything to take the load off you, give you more time to devote to this place. You pay them, for fuck's sake. They'll be earning at the same time as doing what you usually do out there. Your house needs sorting out—it won't be long before it gets dangerous to live here. We've got a hard winter coming on. What if you tell the other men I'm on house duty? That you're paying me to fix it up?"

"I suppose..."

"And as for Macy Jo's." He kissed her soundly before she could say anything then eased back to look down at her. "I don't have to go in with you, but I can wait outside. Look through the window, see if things get nasty. Right?"

She nodded, eyelids growing heavy.

"It's been a bad day, Sarah, honey. How about you go out there and tell the men to take the rest of the day off? I can make sure the horses are stabled. If you go lay on the sofa, you'll be rested enough for tonight." He eased off on holding her so tightly. "Did you feel that?"

"What?" She frowned again.

"There you go again. Making out you don't know what I mean. *That!*" He raised his hips some.

"Uh, yeah. I feel that."

"It isn't just about sex, you know."

"It isn't?"

"Not with me, no. You want me to come clean?"

"If you must."

"Oh, yeah, I must. I've thought about you all day, every day since I first started here. You've gone and burrowed yourself right into my goddamn heart and mind, you know that, woman? I want to care for you, be there for you—if you'll have me."

She smiled a little, looking at him as though she wasn't sure whether to trust. "I might do."

The teasing little— "You might do? So that's how it's going to be, is it?"

"How what's going to be?"

She was trying hard to keep laughter out of her voice, he knew it.

"You keeping me on a string until you decide to let me know where I stand. Where *we* stand."

"Something like that."

"Like I said." He pecked her on the tip of her nose. "All your own way. But, hey, I've waited twelve months already, and I'll wait another twelve, and twelve more if that's what it takes."

"Are you serious?" She cocked her head, her hair bowing with the movement.

"Deadly."

She stared at him, sizing him up if he wasn't mistaken.

"All right!" She straightened her back and shoulders, a proud stance if ever he saw one. "I'm ready to delegate."

"You are?" Well, this was a turn-up for the books. He widened his eyes and suppressed a smile at having won his first victory with her. She might just be seeing shades of grey after all.

"Yes, but if you overstep the mark, you can bet your ass I'll let you know about it."

He laughed again, tucking her hair behind her ear. "I don't doubt that for a second."

"I'm going to lie on the sofa."

"And?"

She pushed away from him and walked to the kitchen doorway. Leaning on the door frame like that, she looked all kinds of sexy and then some.

"And you need to go tell the men to take the rest of the day off. Get one of them to fill in the worksheets for the day before they go."

"Me?" He raised his eyebrows, unable to hide his shock.

"Yes, you. I just changed your job description. Get to it, foreman."

* * * *

Travis walked across the grass towards Clark, thankful that his toe wasn't giving him any trouble. Another shift would see it healed completely. How he'd explain that to Sarah he didn't know, but if he guessed right they'd be taking things slowly, so she wouldn't be seeing him naked any time soon.

The black-haired bastard was giving a mare some exercise in the paddock, a beautiful chestnut with the longest mane Travis had seen in quite a while. Unless he counted Sarah's. The mare's tail swished as she trotted, glinting in the soft rays of the dying sun. The day had been fresh and bright after the storm, the ground drying up like it hadn't taken a beating from the pelting rain the night before.

He watched Clark closely, looking for signs of unease, but found none. Clever bastard knew how to hide his emotions. Despite hating the man, he had to admit Clark had a way with the horses.

He approached the fence, and Clark glanced over, murmuring to the horse and bringing her to a stop. He tied her reins to a post, his arms rigid and bronzed from the hot summer they'd just had. Clark spun to face Travis, and stalked over to lean on the fence.

"What the fuck do you want?" Clark asked.

"Fill this out," Travis said, holding the clipboard up with the worksheet attached.

"Fuck you." Clark presented his back and took a step away.

"I wouldn't walk away from me if you value your job."

Clark halted, spine stiff. Sweat gleamed on his neck, and he clenched his hands into fists. "Like you've got a say in whether I work here or not, asshole."

"I do when I'm your foreman."

Clark flew around, eyes narrowed to slits, mouth a grimace. "You're fucking *what?*"

"You heard me right. So fill this in. Then go home. Early day today." He held the clipboard higher.

Clark hesitated then took it, taking down the pencil he had wedged above his ear. "So that's how it is. New guy gets to be foreman over those of us who've been here longer. What did you do, fuck her into agreeing?"

Travis gritted his teeth.

Clark looked up from writing. "You did, didn't you?"

Was that hatred Travis saw in his eyes?

"No, I didn't. Not all men have to fuck their way through life to get somewhere."

"You taking a pop at me?" Clark sniffed then hawked onto the ground. "Because if you are, you'd better fucking think again. There's people around these parts. People with guns."

"That a threat?"

"It's whatever you want it to be, fucker." Clark thrust the clipboard at Travis.

Travis took it and looked down at his writing. As he knew it would, it matched the note left on Sarah's fridge. "Nice hand you got there. Sheriff Laurie is investigating a note found at Sarah's this morning after a break-in. Very similar. Funny, that."

"Fuck off. You can't prove nothing."

"Not me, no." He left it there, continuing with, "Now go home. I don't want to see you back here until you start work Monday."

Clark opened his mouth to say more but refrained. He pulled open the gate, stalking past Travis, close enough for their jeans to touch. Travis waited a few beats then turned to watch the son of a bitch's retreat...

Then smiled. He'd have that motherfucker's face meeting his fist if it was the last thing he did.

Chapter Six

The old threadbare couch was still comfortable, and its position within the sitting room meant Sarah could lay and watch the developing sunset. The sky was alight with passionate reds and yellows as the sun descended for the day. She was tormented by her thoughts and couldn't resist checking the clock every few minutes.

Sarah was a woman of action. Her father had always taught her to be in their face and show your opponent you weren't scared. That was why she could break and train some of the fiercest horses.

As much as Travis didn't want her facing Clark alone, she would, even surrounded by the asshole's cronies. All she needed was the time and the patience to get out to Macy Jo's bar before Travis got back from touring the ranch. Clark had left in a huff, but not before he'd looked back to the house with a sneer. Sarah had seen the threat on his face and now she was ready to act.

Travis had made it clear he felt something for her and wanted their relationship to be so much more, and deep down she was relieved to have a man around the house—one who'd admitted to caring. But, as much as she liked the revelation and how her body reacted, she must remain a realist.

Why couldn't she tell him she was pleased he'd taken some of the weight off her shoulders? Why couldn't she explain that it was because she wasn't male that she acted the way she did? Oh, she knew it sounded ridiculous now she was a grown woman, to still think of how she'd felt as a young girl, but some things stayed with you no matter how hard you tried to get rid of them. Telling yourself things didn't bother you sometimes didn't work.

When Travis finally decided he'd had enough of banging the boss, he'd leave—move on to the next town and the next bunch of girls. She'd seen it happen to women several times over the years and was determined not to let it happen to her. The town would still be here in his absence and so would she, except her reputation would be ruined. It may be the twenty-first century and all that bollocks, but in a small town, a reputation was the only thing you had going for you. Daddy's was as firm as steel even after his death, and she was determined that hers would be the same.

So she'd keep the change in their relationship quiet for now.

Until it became clear Travis was around to stay.

If that ever happens…

After the last disaster with a boyfriend—which had seen her father threatening the guy with a shotgun—Sarah had taken no more chances. His words stuck with her even today.

"Sarah, I know you want to understand what goes on between a man and a woman, and for some folks it's all

right to do it with everyone they meet. But I want you to remember something. When you give yourself to a person, you're with them for life. They will always hold a part of you. If that man turns out to be a man you don't love, you'll have to live knowing he still holds a part of you. Be sensible, Sarah, and don't settle for second best. I didn't and I'll love your mama until the day I die."

He'd rarely spoken so many words at one time in all of her life, especially words about sex and boys, but those had struck a chord. From that day on, Sarah had stopped running with the pack of girls and didn't make out in the backs of trucks. She'd left school with her virginity intact, while her friends had been pregnant or thinking about settling down and getting married.

The man she would spend the rest of her life with would have every part of her. Old-fashioned views for a modern-day woman, but it was how she would live her life. Travis was the first man she'd ever got so close to wanting. She had urges like every other woman—she'd just learnt to push those urges into her work. Some would say her daddy didn't mean for her to stay a virgin forever, just for a while, but she wasn't old. Twenty-five wasn't old at all.

Was Travis the one? Men had come and tried, but she wouldn't allow just anyone past the wall of ice she'd erected. Her heart was her own, as was her body. Her parents had had a love that lasted a lifetime and she wanted the same.

Which was why she had to go to Macy Jo's tonight, to show the town that she was afraid of nothing and that she was still the same Sarah French who had turned them all down in high school, and would turn them all down now.

The clock struck six, and Sarah moved to the window. Darkness was swallowing up most of the ranch, and she knew how hectic and long the foreman's job was. Travis would be lucky to get back before nine at least. He was nowhere in sight—her plan to be rid of him had worked.

"I'm sorry, Travis, but a woman's got to do what a woman's got to do."

* * * *

An hour later, Sarah went back downstairs dressed in a denim skirt and a tight, white shirt. Using the mirror in the hallway, she painted her lips and puffed out her hair to give it some lift, even though it fell straight back down. Her eyes, already smoky, were now highlighted by black mascara and a small amount of brown eyeshadow—minimal makeup to enhance the beauty, not detract from it. From her working out in the sun all day, her skin shone with a lovely golden tan.

She wrote a short note to Travis, and left a casserole in the oven and some beers chilling in the fridge. Deep down she knew he would follow her, but fingers crossed she'd be back in time before he even knew she'd left. If Clark hadn't broken in, if Travis had gone home at the end of the day as usual, she might have visited Macy Jo's alone anyway.

Ten minutes later, purse in hand, she climbed into her old beat-up truck and took one last look over the fields, wondering if she'd see Travis. The darkness was too thick. The start of winter was fighting back. She smiled at that.

Just like me. Damn straight I'm fighting back.

She started up the truck, the engine growling—another job on her endless list, to get the goddamn truck fixed—and paused, hands on the steering wheel.

Why was she hesitating? She glanced back out at the fields and then to the house. She took a deep breath and went to open the door, the engine still running, thinking she ought to do as Travis said and wait for him.

"What the hell am I doing?" she muttered. "Fuck it!" She slammed the door and revved the engine. "My life, my rules." This was her fight, and she was going to have it sorted once and for all.

She buckled her seatbelt, put the truck in gear, and was on her way.

She refused to look at her rear-view mirror.

This was her life, and she would fuck it up as much or as little as she wanted.

The drive into town was uneventful, the roads quiet at this time of evening. Sarah waved at a few people she recognised while stopping off at the mini-mart to pick up another pack of beer as an apology to Travis. She met a few friendly faces and a couple not so nice, but unfortunately every town had a mix and theirs was no different. Within no time at all she was back in her truck and on the road to Macy Jo's. The popular bar was situated on the outskirts, so not only local folk visited but a few from other towns, and some travellers stopped by for beer and entertainment.

Macy, one of the owners, tried to keep things up and running, hosting events such as birthday parties and novelty events. Sarah was sure Macy had even hosted some rodeo shows.

By seven-thirty it was already busy, and she struggled to find a parking space. She decided to park along the upper bank on the main strip of road, figuring she'd be able to walk the short distance and leave quickly after her mission was complete.

Mission? Was she starting to think she was in some kind of action flick?

She passed men who whistled and did the usual bids for attention. She showed them her precious middle finger and walked into the bar. Beer, sweat and smoke were the smells that invaded her senses. Any other time she would have walked out but instead she took a seat at the bar. Country music blared, and she scanned the room to see if Clark was already here. He wasn't. At least she had time to get herself settled.

Within seconds of her getting comfortable, a guy hit on her.

"Hey, beautiful..."

"Fuck off." Sarah knew how to talk to unwanted suitors.

The man sloped off, not even giving her a second chance to reject. Some men were harder to be rid off and she was in the mood for a fight tonight.

"Well, Sarah French!" Macy squealed as she ran along behind the bar, leaning over and embracing Sarah in a bear hug. "My God, girl, it's been a millennium."

"How are you doing?" Sarah asked once she'd managed to breathe again.

"I'm pregnant again, but me and John are happy."

Macy Jo and John Baines had been high school sweethearts. She knew John was on the same level of cruelty as Clark at times, but with Macy he was like a little teddy bear. Even scary, evil men had their weaknesses.

"Where is John tonight?" Sarah asked.

"At home with the kids. He wanted to be here but the babysitter called in sick. Something to do with the change in the seasons. Anyway, what can I get you to drink?"

"Just a bottle of still water for me, Macy."

Macy's smile dropped.

"What's the matter?" Sarah asked.

"Please… Water? Shit, Sarah, I should have known you'd be here to cause trouble. Whenever you come here and drink water I know you're cruising for a fight. Shit." Macy cursed again, closing her eyes, her lips moving as if in prayer. "I'm calling John." She moved to leave and make the phone call.

"Don't, Macy. I just want some water and some company tonight. I'm not looking for trouble." Under the bar, Sarah crossed her fingers. It was only a small lie. Not really a lie—she wasn't looking for trouble, more like giving out a warning to a creep. Sarah had no intention of ruining everyone's evening or causing any damage to the bar.

She could see Macy didn't believe her so tried her best I'm-a-good-girl-and-all, innocent smile.

It didn't work.

Macy frowned. "I can't afford you messing up my bar. Like I said, you drinking water tells me you're here for trouble. Did you think I'd forget that? With this recession and shit, there really is no money. I'm tied to fuck with this place, and with a baby on the way and all the medical bills…"

"I own a ranch, Macy, and the last I checked I wasn't raking in money. Fuck, I can't even afford to fix my house. I'm not here to cause trouble."

How she hated lying, but it would be up to Clark to decide how things went down.

Macy left to fetch her a bottle of water, giving Sarah time to pace herself. It had been over a year since she'd been here. In fact, the last time had been when her daddy was alive. She understood Macy's concerns. She and Daddy had once caused a little trouble with an outsider who hadn't understood the word no.

"So, now I know you're not causing trouble and are here on a purely chill basis, tell me about that hot little stud Travis Williams. Been a while since I've seen his face in my bar." Macy handed her the water and stayed put.

Sarah was sure she was only staying to keep an eye on her, to watch as she finished her water and left.

"He's good. A good worker." *He's fucking gorgeous, and every time I'm around him I want to forget all my good intentions, drop my panties and fuck his brains out.*

"Yeah, a good worker. All you see in those hard, thick muscles and tempting ass is he's a good worker? Shit, girl, jump on and ride that man. If you don't, other women will be lining up to take him."

Sarah couldn't help but chuckle. It had been some time since she'd felt comfortable enough to laugh. "You're a married woman, Macy Jo. You should be quaint and at home with your husband."

"Why? John admires all the ass in this place. I just know who he keeps coming home to. Looking is not the problem—it's when they start touching that you scream and chop their balls off."

Sarah coughed her water out on the counter, apologising to the people closest. Macy, laughing, handed her some napkins to clean up her mess.

A guy approached Macy and whispered in her ear.

"Oh, shit," Macy said.

"What? What's the matter?" Sarah asked, concerned.

"My life is about to turn to fucking shit," Macy said. "Clark James and some of his group just walked in with a minor." She pointed to the back corner.

Squinting through the layers of smoke, Sarah spotted him. She also spotted Sheriff Laurie. "Why is the sheriff with them?"

"I don't know but I'm getting John here. His mother will have to watch the kids. I have a feeling in my gut things are about to get ugly and I'm not talking about the baby moving, either."

Sarah left the woman to make the phone call and sat watching the group of repulsive men. They all talked amongst themselves, the sheriff looking all goofy as if he belonged with the group. Shit, she'd known not to tell him anything about whom she suspected had broken in to her place. Her instincts had been spot on.

Macy returned, coming out from behind the bar. She stood with Sarah, leaning against it to watch the enemy.

"Why do you think Stephen is with them?" Macy asked.

Sarah knew. She didn't know how, but she had a feeling Clark had found out about the note.

"My house got busted into last night, a sick possessive note left on the refrigerator. Stephen has the note, which is the only piece of evidence left that anyone was even there." Sarah continued to watch the group, her nerves on edge. "Come on, Stephen, walk away," Sarah whispered.

"What the hell is going on?" Macy asked, nodding at the men.

Stephen took the young girl on to the dance floor, getting a little too frisky with the touching and stroking. He was falling for one of the oldest tricks in the book, and Sarah couldn't stand back and let it happen.

"Get the deputy on the phone, Macy. Tell him that Clark James is trying to get Stephen in trouble. Possibly blackmailing him for that note."

"How do you know?"

"That's a minor, and Stephen has evidence which, if proven, can cause problems for Clark. You must have seen something similar to this before? Blackmail with a minor?" *Or maybe I read too many damn crime novels.* "You'll probably find they've got the hotel pre-booked and everything. Just call whoever can help and I'll distract him."

Sarah left her and went on to the dance floor.

The girl was pretty much fake-fucking Stephen on the stage, gyrating against him and pressing her chest into his. Sarah couldn't believe no one was prepared to intervene. She wished she had one of her pistols—she'd show Clark a thing or two, limey bastard that he was.

"Baby, I think it's time you danced with a real woman," Sarah purred. She pulled the minor off and moved into place, Stephen's wobbly arms surrounding her. The alcohol and smoke fumes came off him in waves, the stench overpowering.

"Hello, Sarah," he yelled into her ear.

He really was drunk, possibly even drugged. The guy was sweating something bad.

"Hello, Stephen." She smiled but looked around for Macy or John. Neither was in sight, so she continued to dance. "What are you doing here?"

He started to lean to one side, and she had to use both arms around his waist to hold him steady.

"Wanted a drink."

In other words, Clark had coerced him down here. So he was being manipulated just like all the other times before he'd become sheriff. Where were this guy's balls? Clark was probably twiddling them in his fist.

"I've lost your letter...evidence," he slurred.

There's the answer.

Sarah chanced a look at the back of the room. Clark was still in the same place. The hair on the back of her neck stood on end, everything about the situation telling her to retreat.

"Clark wants you bad," Stephen said.

"He can't have me, and Stephen—you're the sheriff. You should protect me. Not be standing here drunk and dancing with a minor. Don't you see what he's trying to do?"

"A minor? Damn well looks old enough. She wanted my company."

"The girl attends the local high school, you should know that. You carry on with her and you'll be in jail or worse. Blackmailed by Clark, right? For fuck's sake, Stephen, think!" She struggled to hold her panic in check. It seemed she couldn't handle this situation on her own, and it hurt to admit that even to herself.

A rasping voice Sarah hated broke into her thoughts.

"I think I should cut in here, buddy."

Sarah tensed, knowing she was cornered. She whirled around.

Clark stood in her personal space.

"She's all yours, Clark," Stephen said, ambling back towards the girl.

Sarah made to turn, but Clark grasped her waist in his claws. She glared at him and tried to move out of his way.

"Let go of me," she demanded.

"I don't think so."

He spun her around the small room, and people just ignored them, his touch at her waist bruising as she continued to fight with him to leave her alone. This had been a really bad idea, and now she wished she'd done exactly what Travis had told her and stayed at home. Safe and sound.

"You smell nice, Sarah," he said into her ear, breath hot.

"Stay away from me, you repulsive bastard."

"Feisty little bitch. I wonder if Travis likes that about you."

"Whatever he likes, it's none of your business."

She looked for Macy and saw her biting her fingernail, nerves clearly on edge. Macy gave her apologetic eyes that told her neither the deputy nor John had arrived yet. Fuck, this evening was turning into a nightmare.

She wanted home and a hot bath ASAP.

And Travis.

"You know, there was a wolf on your property last night," Clark drawled.

Frowning, Sarah turned her attention back to the man holding her. "What?"

"A wolf looking through your window. I shot the little fucker in the foot before he could get any closer. That kind of protection deserves some sort of reward, don't you think?"

She knew what he meant. His thoughts repulsed her.

"You were on my property? I could have you done for trespassing."

"I work there, darlin', and any judge in the county would see it as me doing a young woman a favour. They might even reward me."

Travis had been shot in the foot. *Travis* was outside her house in the rain. Travis couldn't be a wolf—what the fuck was Clark talking about? He was lying, trying to goad her into something. Or trying to get out of admitting he'd shot Travis. She held back a retort, one that would have shown him how pissed off he'd made her. She didn't want that.

"Maybe we should go somewhere now and you can show your appreciation with your mouth," Clark said.

Sarah couldn't stop the disgust she felt inside appearing on her face. She grimaced, eyes narrowed. His revolting suggestion made her sick to her stomach.

"Get your fucking hands off me." She slapped him around the face, throwing herself away from him.

The bar went silent in between songs. She felt as though everyone had seen her attack him yet they stood by and did nothing. She fell to the floor, stumbling in her ridiculous high heels.

"I don't think the lady wants you, buddy." A man—a stranger to town—approached in an attempt to protect Sarah, and got a bloodied nose and thrust into the crowd for his trouble.

The room went on tense alert as the man came back towards Clark with his fists raised, about to return a few punches of his own. Clark's cronies brought out guns and weapons as a warning. Shit, this was going from bad to fucking worse, and all Sarah could do was remain sprawled on the damn floor like a helpless girl.

Get the hell up and get out of here!

She remained in place, rooted as she watched the scene unfolding before her.

"Now, now," Clark said when the man was nearly upon him. "This is our town, and we don't want to start causing trouble. This is none of your business. Back off."

He'd spoken clearly and surely, and the stranger must have seen by the glint in Clark's eyes that he'd be better off walking away. He cupped his nose and retreated back to his table, consoled by a thin man in a Stetson. Had it really been that long since she'd come into town for a social visit? Clark had been a blip on the radar last time she'd checked.

Sarah managed to get up as Clark moved towards her. He grabbed her arms, holding her in a dead lock, and she brought her knee up, slamming it into his dick. He released her with a pained grunt.

"I said, don't fucking touch me! And if you come into my house again I'll cut your fucking dick off," she warned.

"Yeah, who's going to stop me?"

"I am." Everyone turned towards the voice who'd challenged Clark.

Standing in the doorway, looking menacing and sexy as sin, was Travis Williams, her protector, ready for a fight.

Chapter Seven

Travis stared at Clark, hands balled, the need to connect them to the man's body an insistent urge. "You'd better fuck the hell off out of here, if you know what's good for you."

Clark smirked, turned to fully face Travis and sucked in a noisy breath, chest filling with air. He looked ridiculous, the way he tried to pump himself up as some indestructible force.

Indestructible, my ass.

"You're not my foreman here, asshole." Clark smiled, a nasty grin that contorted his face. He narrowed his eyes and stretched his lips wider, the bottom one glistening with spittle. Sweat broke out on his face, giving him a disgusting wet sheen. "So dishing out orders isn't quite gonna cut it. I'm off the clock. No work rules apply here in Macy Jo's. Nothing applies here other than having a good time, friends meeting with friends, people chilling out after a hard week's work." He glanced around, nodding at everyone in turn, gaze finally settling on Macy as though he dared her to refute his claim. "The people here know I'm minding my own business, having a drink with my buddies." He gestured to the whole room. "This woman here, she just got the wrong end of the stick is all."

"That woman," Travis said, "is your *boss*. And, from where I'm standing, she got the *right* end of the stick. You need to understand when a woman says no she means no and leave her the fuck alone."

"Yeah, yeah, whatever. Women say no, but us men, we all know they mean yes. Just being coy, that's what they are." Clark waved a hand in dismissal and swivelled to rejoin his cronies.

The ball of anger in Travis' gut grew tighter. What the hell was up with this guy? What part of 'get off me' didn't he understand? How could he go around like he did, disregarding people's feelings and doing whatever the fuck he liked, bullying the townsfolk into standing by his side? When had he discovered his power over them? Or had he always been like this? Clark had lived here all his life, and Travis had no trouble imagining the younger Clark terrorising the neighbourhood until people just did whatever they could to appease him.

Travis held a hand out to Sarah, who walked over to him on unsteady legs, although she straightened her spine and lifted her chin. Dignified, even in the worst and most embarrassing of circumstances. Shit, he admired her so much. She stood by his side, and he settled one hand at the base of her spine, feeling her well-concealed shivers.

Clark had a lot to answer for.

"Clark," she called, voice surprisingly strong and even.

The bastard glanced at her over his shoulder, putting one hand on his hip. "What?"

"You know you mentioned Travis being your foreman?"

"Yeah? So what?" He scowled, bowing his arms at his sides as though he wanted to punch her.

"He isn't," she said.

What? She was taking away Travis' new title? What the fuck had he done now?

"Good." Clark turned to face her. "Glad to see you've got a snippet of sense inside that tiny brain of yours. I was beginning to wonder."

Travis stepped forward, nausea swirling inside him at the blatant rudeness of the man. "If you so much as say one more word like that to her again I'll—"

"He isn't your foreman," Sarah interjected, voice loud, "because you're fired. I don't want to see your smarmy little ass anywhere near my ranch. I'll send one of the guys over with any wages you're owed. No one touches me like you did. No one speaks to me that way." She paused, glaring at Clark with spite in her eyes. "And, just so you know, I have a gun in every damn room—and I'm not afraid to use them."

"You fucking bitch whore," Clark snarled, striding towards her. "You're going to regret ever speaking to me like that."

He reached her quickly, lifting his hands, fingers splayed, claw-like.

Travis nudged Sarah backwards and stepped between them. "Fuck the hell off or so help me God I'll hammer you. Accept what the lady said and move on."

He shoved Clark's chest, but the man didn't flinch or move.

"Lady? Fucking *lady?*" Clark laughed, showing yellowed teeth, the two front ones chipped on opposing corners. "She ain't no damn lady. She's a bitch on two legs—legs she'd open for anyone given half the chance."

Travis didn't understand how Clark had arrived at that conclusion, but he didn't give it another thought. His body took over his mind, one fist rising to connect with Clark's jaw. Clark fell backwards, into a surge of his friends who'd no doubt anticipated things were going to end up this way. He fought to right himself, cheeks a red blaze, eyes snapping anger.

"You motherfucking—" Clark spluttered, pushed to his feet by several pairs of hands. He shucked them away, slapping behind him. "Get the hell off me, jerks. I don't need your help. I'm well able to look after myself."

He lunged forward, head down, in place to ram Travis in the gut. Travis sidestepped and Clark sailed on, crashing into two bar stools then coming to rest as a sprawling heap on the floor. Travis eyed him, waiting for the madman to spring back on to his feet and take another pop. Clark remained where he was, a tangle of arms and legs, breath coming out of him in fast, sharp bursts.

"*You* had better fuck off out of here," Clark rumbled, "before I get up."

"Why?" Travis asked. "Reckon you can take me on?"

"Yeah, and you know it. Take you on and finish you the fuck up." Clark hawked and spat, wiping his mouth with the back of one hand.

"That a threat?"

Travis waited for an answer of denial. No way was Clark stupid enough to admit anything in front of a bar full of rapt people.

"Yeah, that's a threat all right." He stared, irises turning dark, his mouth a sideward bracket. "One I'll hold good. If I see you, wolf boy, you'd better run."

Scrub him not being stupid enough… And fuck! 'Wolf boy'…

"So do it now," Travis said. "May as well get on with it while the going's good, while you're angry. Or are you too spent to get up and deal with me right now? Hurt yourself going down, did you? Is that it? You trying to save face? Fucking pansy."

Maybe he shouldn't have goaded the man, but he couldn't help himself. Better they sorted their differences now, put an end to the feud and drew a line under it. With witnesses. Travis was angry—shit, was he angry—but Travis reckoned he could hold off shifting while in a tussle with Clark. If he allowed himself to teeter on the brink of changing, he'd get the extra strength he needed to teach this prick a lesson—that messing with Travis—or Sarah—wasn't the best thing Clark had chosen to do.

"Nah." Clark sat up, in no hurry to get to his feet. He planted his palms on the floor behind him and leant back, looking for all the world like he was having a bit of relaxation time. "I prefer leaving you in suspense. You know, looking over your shoulder. And then, when you least expect it, going in for the kill while your guard's down, your woman's alone, ready for me to visit."

Travis shook his head, the mention of Sarah being alone revealing Clark's intentions hadn't changed. He still planned to make her his, whatever the cost. He wasn't going to give up. Sarah wasn't interested, and everyone here had seen that but… Travis had no doubt the guy knew exactly how Sarah felt about him, but he didn't care.

What Clark wanted, Clark got, simple as that.

Not this time.

"You heard that, right?" Travis said loudly, appealing to the crowd. "You heard what he's got in mind? Something he's had in mind before tonight. Reckons he's going to force himself on Sarah. Any of you got a problem with that?"

No one responded, just stared back at him with blank faces.

"What the hell is up with you people? How can you support a jerk like him?" He kept Clark in his peripheral, making sure he'd spot him the minute the bastard made a move.

Still no response.

"Stephen?" Travis looked at the sheriff, far gone on alcohol by the looks of him. "You don't do anything about threats these days? You hang out with guys who make them now?"

Stephen shrugged.

"You'd better watch you don't lose your job, Sheriff," Travis said, "or worse, hanging out with the likes of him." He jerked his thumb in Clark's direction.

Why wasn't Clark getting up? Why the hell was he allowing people to see him down like that? It went against everything Travis knew about the man—someone who always showed himself as hard, able to take care of himself. Before tonight, if Travis had been told Clark was acting submissive in body, if not in speech, he'd never have believed them. Did he want everyone to see he wasn't going to fight, wasn't the one causing trouble here? The innocent party despite his threats?

Clever bastard has it all worked out.

Met with silence and stares once more, Travis looked back to Clark. "You'd better not show up on Sarah's land again. I see you there..." He thought back to what he'd told Sarah he'd do. "I'll rip your fucking throat out. And that isn't a threat but a goddamn promise." He turned from Clark's sneering face and back to Stephen. "You hear that, Sheriff? I just threatened your new buddy. Don't you reckon you need to do something about it?"

Stephen reddened, shuffling his feet and looking to Clark for guidance. Where had the old Stephen gone? How had he been replaced by this insipid yes-man in a matter of hours? Jesus, he'd only seen Stephen this morning, and he'd been his usual self—ready to work and solve a crime, helping Sarah with the break-in.

He been slipped drugs or something?

The bar was silent except for breathing and the occasional shifted foot.

"Aww, fuck you all. I can see what's going on here," Travis said, taking Sarah's elbow. "Good luck in your small-minded worlds, led by a small-minded prick. And if something happens to me—or Sarah—maybe your consciences will prickle hard enough for you to stand up against a man who seems to have you all dangling on his hook. Come on." He guided Sarah to the door, on alert that Clark might take this moment to jump up and attack.

He pushed the door open, allowing Sarah to walk out first.

No attack. No sounds of movement. No sounds at all.

Bunch of fucking bastards.

Outside, he walked Sarah to her car on the rise, hand on her back. "Can you give me a lift to my place, honey?"

She frowned at him, one half of her face lit by the overpowering lilac, neon light shining from Macy Jo's gaudy sign—a four-foot tall, half-nude cowgirl flashing her tits. "You didn't come here by truck?"

"Uh, no. I ran." *Shit.* He'd stripped, put his clothes in a rucksack, shifted, then carried the bag in his mouth all the way here. The backpack was stowed under a bush—he could pick it up another time.

"Ran? Jesus, you're crazy. That's one hell of a way on foot." Her frown deepened, then the creases completely disappeared from her forehead. "I'm not sorry I came here, you know."

"I didn't think you would be." He stroked her hair, loving yet hating her impulsiveness all at the same time.

"I'm sorry it got out of hand, that he pushed himself on me like that, and I'm sorry I lost a friend but—"

"Lost a friend?"

She nodded, gaze straying to the bar door then roving the sign, sadness in her eyes. "Macy. She called for the deputy and John—damn lot of good that did, they didn't show—but when you spoke to them all like that..." She sighed then swallowed. "She never stood up and said anything. She's as scared of Clark as everyone else. That or she's so down in trade even his cash is welcome."

"Ah, fuck. I'm sorry you had to see that. She'll call, try to explain, I'm sure." He rubbed her back.

"I don't care if she does. I won't be answering it." She clamped her jaw.

"Now that's just silly." He sighed, wondering if she'd ever see things from someone else's point of view over her own. He cared for her deeply, but that trait of hers drove him crazy.

"Call how I feel silly again and you'll be running back home as well." She unlocked her car and opened the door.

"Sorry. I didn't mean—"

"I know, I know. Just get in, will you?"

She didn't take him to his place, instead driving right past the turn, continuing towards her ranch. Travis never said a word. He'd much rather be with her, keeping her close, than roaming about as a wolf outside. Although the rain had stopped, the air had a distinct nip to it that even his pelt wouldn't fully keep out. Yeah, being inside, albeit in her spare room, held greater appeal.

As her car trundled on, he let his anger cool to a simmer, trying to see things rationally. He thought of Clark the last time he'd seen him, vulnerable on the floor like that. Now Travis knew what the man was playing at, what he had in mind, he'd prepare himself for an attack. Although Clark had said he liked keeping people in suspense, Travis just couldn't believe he'd be afforded the same option. Could Clark leave things as they were for God knew how long, watching Travis manage the men and being close to Sarah? Was he that wily, that prepared to wait?

No, Clark would do something and do it soon. What, though, he had no idea. Maybe he'd sneak into the house again one night, overpowering Travis and taking Sarah against her will—two birds with one stone.

The thought sent him cold.

As they pulled up to the ranch house, Sarah cut the engine and got out, tossing the keys onto the seat for Travis to lock up with. He did, rushing so he could scope the perimeter and go inside the house before she did. He wanted to check every damn nook and cranny. She wasn't pleased about her control being usurped, her frown and *tsk* of disapproval told him that, but he didn't care. He was going to take care of her, seeing as she wasn't in a rush to take care of herself. Allowing her to trail behind him as he searched the rooms—he'd rather that than leave her alone outside—he proclaimed it safe as they returned to the kitchen.

"You want me to stay?" he asked.

Better to make sure than assume.

"If you like."

She busied herself filling the kettle, getting mugs out for tea, and he sat at the table watching her jerky movements while keeping an ear cocked for strange sounds outside. What he wouldn't give to find out why she was so…so fucking *obstinate*. If she told him, he could maybe help her through it, find ways for her to cope without being so abrupt and icy. Hell, he'd heard tell throughout his life that women were an enigma, but this one was the queen. He resisted asking any questions, thinking he ought to just be quiet until she offered conversation.

She didn't, thudding a mug of tea onto the table in front of him and plonking herself into a chair opposite. She cupped her mug with both hands, and he studied her face for signs of stress. They were there all right—tight lines beside the corners of her mouth and eyes half-lidded from the frown that seemed to live permanently on her brow—and he longed to make them go away.

"So, we're one man short," she said. "I'll put an advertisement in the paper."

So that's how she was going to play it, was it? Sweep what had happened under the damn carpet, let it fester in her head, keeping her emotions tightly under wraps. Had he expected anything less?

"All right," he said, letting her lead the way. If he pushed, he'd likely meet up with a fucking high brick wall. "We'll manage well enough without him. If we're honest, Clark had a habit of making it look like he was busy while in reality he did fuck all. We'll continue the same way without him, getting the same amount of work done, I'll bet." He sipped some tea.

"So you think it's pointless taking on a new man, is that what you're saying?" She stared at the tabletop as though it offended her, like she wanted to kill it…or someone.

"No, I'm not saying your suggestion is pointless." Was he really in the mood for another argument with her? He bit back a sigh in case *that* pissed her off as well. "What I meant was, we can manage just as well until a new guy comes along."

"Right."

She sipped, he sipped—sipped until their damn mugs were empty and the kitchen was full of tension. About to call it a night—it was obvious Sarah wasn't going to offload her worries—Travis stood and stretched.

"Take me to bed?" she asked, still murdering the tabletop with her stare.

Her suggestion startled the shit out of him, and he lowered his arms, looking down at her with his mouth gaping. Did she just want him to fuck the night out of her, erase everything that had happened so she only had him and what they were doing to think about?

Or did she actually want *him?*

Chapter Eight

What the fuck did I just say?

Sarah supposed her request should have come with at least a little eye contact. Did she even want to give herself to him? Never before in her life had she been so relieved to see a man than when she'd seen Travis standing in that bar doorway. She knew deep down how scared they all were of Clark, and it was so stupid because Clark was a big dumb loser, his cronies' loyalty the only thing going for him.

She shuddered.

"I'd better go," Travis said.

He moved to leave, jolting her out of her reverie and into action. Sarah only had Travis in this world and she wasn't going to let him go. Her daddy had told her she'd know when she met the right man—and she was sure Travis was that man.

She reached out, catching his arm. "Please don't leave."

His shoulders slumped, and he turned back towards her. Her heart beat frantically. What could she do? Lay on her back with her legs open and demand to be fucked? What was the correct procedure for suggesting intercourse other than what she'd already done—asking outright? Great, now she was sounding like some sort of teacher.

Get your shit together!

"I want you to stay." Licking her lips, she placed one of his hands against her breast.

Instead of him taking over, he just stared at his hand on her body.

"Please, Travis," she said.

He swallowed then pulled his hand away—*he* didn't move away, though, but settled her in his arms, taking her lips in a brutal kiss. His lips were hard and bruising as he controlled her body, forcing her to accept his tongue, weakening her defences with his explosive kiss.

He moved his mouth from her lips and down her neck, sucking at her collarbone. She whispered his name, sensations bombarding her virgin body. He sunk his fingers into the thick strands of her hair.

Her knees buckled as he circled her waist with his other arm, holding her steady.

"You taste so good," he growled, pulling away.

Sarah whimpered with longing, wanting his lips all over her body.

"Do you really want this, Sarah?"

His question was so stupid—she didn't want anything else—but she was thankful for his concern, for making sure she knew what she wanted. She nodded, the only movement she was capable of doing.

She expected him to take her hand and lead her to the bedroom to make long, slow, leisurely love, where he kissed her into sweet oblivion. Instead, he thrust her against the nearest wall, his actions animalistic as he tore at her clothes. She was surprised at how turned on she was by his aggressiveness. A thrill surged through her, and her cunt grew wet, nipples perking to the point of pain. Her shirt and short denim skirt were disposed of within seconds until she stood in her simple bra and panties, surprisingly unselfconscious, proudly showing him what she had to offer.

"Take your bra off," he demanded, removing his shirt and jeans.

Her pussy responded to all of the glorious muscles on display. She wanted to lick every square inch of him, to feel his warm skin on hers, his hands roving her body, his mouth doing the same. She wanted... God, she wanted so much, all at the same time, and her head lightened with the assault of sensations and thoughts bombarding her.

What would his arms feel like beneath her palms as he grabbed her hips and thrust inside her? Would it hurt? She'd ridden horses all her life, knew her hymen could have been broken years ago, but having a solid cock inside her... And from the look of the bulge in his underwear, his cock was a generous size.

She rid her mind of those thoughts and her body of the obstructive bra, her breasts falling out, heaving as she took each indrawn breath.

Travis reached out, cupping each breast, his thumbs running round her tight nipples. She bowed her head back, and he circled one nipple with his lips, still caressing the other with his thumb. Sarah crossed her legs, her pussy demanding attention, her clit swollen and pulsing. She was on fire for more. He lifted her up, and on instinct she wrapped her legs around his waist, his thick cock seating between her pussy lips.

They panted and moaned, holding each other, lavishing attention on their bodies.

"I want you, Travis," she cried, thrusting and grinding her slit on his black, brief-covered cock.

A rending tear and her panties were gone. How had he managed to move as fast as he did?

'A wolf looking through your window. I shot the little fucker in the foot before he could get any closer…'

Clark's words invaded her mind. Wolf and speed… She shook her head, not wanting the image intrusion of such a creature. She wanted Travis—her heart, mind and body needed this man. He called to the part of her she'd kept long-buried underneath layers and layers of attitude. To finally sense her true self again, so close to the surface, dying to get out… She was adamant not to let her go again.

She deserved to be a woman. To crave love and sex and all the delightful sins in between.

"I want you, baby. I'll always want you," Travis rasped.

His words were wonderful to hear. Sarah leant down and kissed him, savouring the feel of his tongue on hers, the heat of it as he explored her mouth, the thrill of it zipping pleasure right down to her cunt. He reached down to pull himself free of his briefs, aligned his cock with her entrance, and she opened her mouth to warn him, to tell him…

He stared into her eyes and thrust home.

His unbelievable speed halted her warning, and, before she could stop the reaction, Sarah screamed in pain. Her mind and body were ready to accept the pleasure, but he was too wide and thick. An unbearable sharp pain and fiery burn took the pleasure out of it. She sunk her nails into his skin, marking his flesh. Tears sprang to her eyes and she sobbed.

This was not supposed to happen. She should be on a wave of bliss and happiness.

"Shit, fucking hell," he cursed.

He stilled all movement and hugged her tight, breath ragged. Sarah laid her head against his neck, her eyes closed while she grew accustomed to his length and width. He stroked her hair and soothed her with kind words, his tenderness making her fall in love with him just that little bit more.

"You should have told me, honey."

He didn't move but held her tighter, his cock still hard and strong. Every movement he made created an answering kick of pain in her body.

"I forgot… Going too fast…" She couldn't look at him and see the pity in his eyes.

"I never knew you would be untouched. I assumed… I thought you… Shit!" He kissed her cheek. "I'm honoured to be your first, honey."

Sarah already knew in her heart he would be her last. Never again would she allow a man to get this close to her. She loved being in his arms and feeling his love as he calmed and relaxed the ache within her.

"I'm sorry," she mumbled, the sound muffled by his neck. "I'm on the pill, if that makes you feel better." She flushed at her admission then went on quickly to cover her embarrassment. "In case, you know, you were wondering. I have terrible cramps. The pills help. I'm not on it because I want to sleep around, I—"

"Shh. It's okay. You don't need to explain. You want me to carry on? Are you all right? Does it hurt?"

"It's okay. I'm okay."

"I'm going to start moving. Tell me right away if you need me to stop. I've got you. Just hold me, baby. Let me do the work."

Even though it was hurting a little, she didn't want him to stop. Sarah had wanted him to be her first for a long time. He was the only man she'd ever trust with something so precious.

She tightened her hold around his neck. He walked slowly, and she didn't think about her naked body exposed to the air or the fact that a naked man was carrying her naked ass upstairs.

The movements made his cock jolt, still seated inside her, and now, like in all of those cheesy romance books she'd read in her teens, her pussy was starting to become accustomed to his size and length.

In her bedroom, he walked them to the side of the bed. "I'm going to lay you down. Do this the way it should have been done for your first time."

"Don't leave me." Sarah held him in place with her arms, at the same time clamping her legs to stop him leaving her. "Don't pull out." She may have been in pain with the first thrust, but already her body was awakening to something more. She had a feeling, if he withdrew then pushed into her afresh, she'd go through that burn again. She rubbed her clit against his pubis, the fine hairs teasing every delightful pull inside her body.

"I don't want to hurt you." He laid a kiss on the corner of her mouth.

She smiled to show him she was all right. "It's okay. Please…" The discomfort was easing, the pain bearable now, and her smile turned wicked. "Fuck me, foreman." Her dark side was coming forth, giving her the courage to continue. She didn't have any prior practice in this area but reading a few soppy romances seemed to have helped.

He chuckled, making his cock lunge further inside her now-dripping channel. Sarah gasped, thrusting down to meet him. He manoeuvred them onto the bed.

"That's it, Sarah, show me how much you want me," he dared.

She was never one to turn down a challenge. Sarah moved her hips, dancing underneath him, using all of the knowledge she'd gained from books and the odd few documentaries as well. As embarrassing as it was to admit, watching the horses mate around breeding time was coming to good use. She cried out when he moved up, taking her hips in his hands and pushing himself fully into her.

Quickly, he shifted them around so he lay beneath her. The change of position increased the burn in her channel, and she sucked in a breath as his tip pushed into something tender at the top.

"Ride me," he commanded, holding her waist, lifting her up and down, showing her what he wanted her to do.

Sarah followed his lead, watching and learning, her body coming alight under his experienced hands.

"Touch your breasts for me."

Nervous, but at the same time exhilarated, wanting to do whatever he asked, she touched her full mounds. Using her fingertips, she circled each nipple, thrumming and stroking. He pressed one hand to her stomach and, inch by glorious inch, moved it down until two of his fingers touched her swollen nub. She arched her back, the pleasure consuming her once his fingers continued to stroke the sensitive bundle of nerves.

"Come for me, Sarah?"

Her body tightened, her inner walls clenching around him, bliss beginning in her clit then growing to a full-on assault of raging pleasure. It spread, and she was hard pressed to keep riding him, unused to coping with two things like this at once. She moved her hands from her breasts and tucked them beneath him, holding his ass as the wave of pleasure completely took over, driving her crazy. He circled his hips, cock plunging, and continued caressing her clit. The dual sensation of his cock and fingers was more than she could handle. She dug her nails into his skin, clawing at him the moment the peak of her climax washed over her.

Sarah couldn't see, couldn't think past the bolts of lust striking her. He worked her clit past the climax, demanding more from her body. She opened her legs wider, allowing him room to drive harder and faster.

He reached down and pulled her hands free, taking them in his and holding them above her head in one hand. He took one of her legs and pulled it higher against his body, her knee nestled close to his armpit. The scissor effect almost had her crying out at the quick stab of pain in her cunt, but she gritted her teeth and rode through it—determined, as with everything else she did, to get through this her way and without showing weakness. She fucked him hard and fast and didn't have time to come down from one climax before she was hurtling headlong into another release from her clit rubbing his coarse hairs, the sensations stronger and more powerful than before.

"Please, Travis," she begged as she came down from the high, but she didn't know what she was begging for, what she wanted. Did she want him to stop?

It felt so good with his dick inside her.

Travis kissed her, sweat shining on his skin, and, by instinct, Sarah knew he was about to climax. His cock throbbed, seemed to grow in width and length for a breath-hitching moment, and he rolled his eyes. His body jerked, no longer controlled by him, and became a mass of movement.

"You're so fucking beautiful," he growled.

With a final thrust down, Sarah felt his cock pulsing, then his seed exploding. Wet heat flooded her as his climax continued to spurt.

"Jesus, fuck!" he said, gripping her waist, fingertips pressing into her flesh. "Stop, honey. Please stop. I can't..."

She eased to a halt, looking down at him, worried she'd hurt him or had done something wrong.

He looked up at her. "It's okay, honey. I'm just tender. You'll learn when to stop, because I plan on us doing this a whole lot more. God, woman, you fuck like a dream."

She smiled, so damn pleased with herself, and braced for more pain as she lifted off him. Thankfully, it was just soreness from being stretched, and she settled by his side where they rested, panting in each other's arms.

* * * *

Sarah woke when Travis carried her through to the bathroom, her heart melting upon seeing light from several candles burning around the tub. The sweet scent of bath soaps filled the air.

"You didn't have to do this," she whispered, nuzzling his neck, wondering how she'd got so goddamn lucky.

"I wanted to. You deserve the world." He lowered her into the bath, turning on some soothing music to play in the background.

Moments later, he climbed in and settled behind her, his arms circling her waist. She let her head fall back on to his shoulder.

"Did I hurt you?" he asked.

She shook her head, too busy looking around and trying not to over-think all of his hard work. It would be so easy to love this man…

Her heart stuttered. It wouldn't *be* so easy—it *was* easy. She didn't understand how it had happened but it had. Maybe she'd grown to love him over the past year, confusing that emotion with friendship. She looked down into the bubble-soaked water and knew her heart was owned, and would only ever be owned, by this man.

"I'm so sorry, baby. I never meant to hurt you. I had no idea…"

Sarah, shocked by her thoughts, jolted at his words. "You didn't hurt me, Travis. On the contrary, you finally made me *feel*."

It was the truth. Before Travis Williams had entered her life she'd been a shell of a woman and now she was alive and ready for more.

"Let me care for you?" he asked, taking a cloth and dropping it into the water.

Sarah moaned. She couldn't bear to talk and allow her long-held emotions to close round the moment and strangle it. She knew Travis cared, but with the opening of her heart, she knew it would terrify her to let him know what she was thinking and feeling too soon. To be vulnerable to anyone would be the hardest thing in the world. What would she do if she was to wake up alone now? To find out all Travis wanted was a quick tumble with the ice-queen ranch owner? That it had all been a deliberate ruse, with him using her as she'd feared? She was young, she was sure she would get over it if this turned out to be true, but would her life ever be the same?

She watched him move from her back to between her legs, leaning her head against the bath tub. He took the cloth in one hand and her foot in the other and lathered her leg and insole with warm, soapy water. She groaned at the touch, lifting her leg as he followed the cloth all the way up and down. Once one leg was thoroughly washed and cleansed he moved on to the other. She'd never dreamt it was possible to become aroused while someone washed her. Every time he turned his gaze on her, she didn't know how to explain the tight heat in her stomach and her cunt, shooting from those points and throughout her body.

"What are you doing?" she asked, gasping when the devil of a cloth touched right against her heat.

He replaced the wet fabric with his hand, his thumb pressing on her pulsing womanhood while his fingers sought the entrance to her pussy.

"I don't want you to stop thinking about me," he said, thrusting two fingers inside. "I want to be the only man who fills your head and your cunt. The only man who you want to wake up with every day and the one you want to kiss goodnight."

Sarah held on to the sides of the tub, closed her eyes, her body becoming alive with his passionate onslaught.

"I could never stop thinking about you," she confessed.

He licked a trail up to her mouth and she gasped. Already attuned to Travis and what he wanted, she opened up to receive him.

'A wolf looking through your window. I shot the little fucker in the foot before he could get any closer…'

Why was that goddamn man's voice penetrating her mind whenever Travis came close to making her feel like a quivering mess?

She responded to the threat of those words, tightening up, and the pleasure stopped instantly. She silently cursed Clark and the shitty horse he'd ridden in on. The bastard needed to learn to stay the hell away from her—and her thoughts.

"What's the matter, honey?"

She loved hearing Travis' endearments but needed to ask a question, otherwise she could imagine Clark and his irritating voice fucking over her future intimacy with this man. Clark's words echoed in her mind again.

"Oh, for fuck's sake," she said through clenched teeth, then sat up to splash her face with water and tried to clear her mind.

"Did I do something?" Travis asked.

She wiped her face and shook her head. "Not. It's not you. It's something Clark said. I keep hearing it."

His eyebrows shot up and he grinned. "My fingers were buried deep inside your hot pussy and you're thinking about that fucking loser?"

Okay—said like that, it sounded damn awful.

"I can't get what he said out of my mind." She bit her lip. It would sound so stupid if she asked him.

"Tell me so we can get it out of the way."

She frowned, shaking her head. *It's so stupid.*

"About a wolf being outside my house," she said quickly and waited to see if he gave it any serious response.

"I didn't see a wolf."

Aggravated now, thinking she was losing her mind, allowing that bastard to make her feel this way, she just came out with it. "He said he shot a wolf in the foot. Travis, you were shot in the foot."

He was also in the bath and didn't appear to have a scratch on him.

"Are you trying to say I'm a wolf?"

She detected the humour in his words and wanted to beat him with a big stick. Saying the words out loud had sounded ludicrous.

"No… Yes… I don't know." Placing her head in her hands, she didn't have the first clue what to do. Make a joke of it? After all, was she seriously considering Travis being a wolf? People didn't change into animals, she wasn't stupid. How had she let Clark make her ponder such a dumb thing?

"No," she said. "I don't think you're a wolf. Stupid of me to bring it up."

"Okay, now that's settled, let me wash you and then carry you to bed where I can make love to you every way possible."

What woman in the world would argue with that?

He massaged her muscles as he washed her, going slowly, driving her insane. He heated up her body, a sure-fire way to make her want more. By the time he carried her through to the bedroom, Sarah wanted to be loved and fucked for hours.

Travis kissed every inch of her, shocking and delighting her as he opened her legs with his callused hands and moments later made his tongue dance between her wet folds. She cried out, sinking her fingers into his hair, her body whirling along the peak of pleasure. He pierced her folds with his tongue, pushing it inside her channel, making it feel as though he made love to every part of her at once. Her mind grew wicked with every movement he made, the wanton side of her begging to be set free.

He rested her legs over his shoulders, drinking her in. She couldn't stop watching. Everything he was doing made her want him more. Her release was quick and strong, and he fed his cock to her cunt while still controlling her climax with his fingers, her walls tightening as he pushed inside.

This time he made love to her for hours. Slowness by agonising slowness, he took her, and Sarah enjoyed and loved every second.

Travis rolled over, taking her with him, allowing her to ride him at her own pace. Sarah gasped. He was deeper and she could take as much or as little of him as she wanted. He rested his hands on her hips, helping but not controlling. He was under her power and she used it to the best of her ability. Watching his reactions became like a drug. She wanted to see him lose his mind the way he'd made her lose hers.

"Shit, Sarah, faster," he cried out.

She leant down, kissing him, and before she knew what was happening he had her under him and had slammed all of himself inside her.

He moves so fast…

Crying out together, they let go. Sarah fell and fell hard, and not just through climax and the heat.

She fell headlong in love with the man in her arms.

Chapter Nine

Travis awoke, instantly alert. Some fucker was outside, he knew it. He lay in the darkness, staring at the shadowy ceiling, his heart thumping, and strained his ears to hear even the slightest of sounds. Sarah's steady breathing filled the air around him. His pulse quickened, the throb of it almost drowning her breath out.

There it was again—the noise he must have heard while sleeping. Like metal being clanked. Keys, maybe? A chain being rattled? He eased out of bed, mindful not to wake Sarah. The last thing he wanted was for her to spring up, panicked that Clark had returned. No, she needed a good night's sleep, not one disturbed by Travis' possibly overactive imagination.

Who was he kidding? He'd heard that sound all right, no doubt about it.

He moved over to the window, wincing at the sound of his feet rasping against the floor, and slowly drew the edge of one curtain across, giving him just enough space to peer out to the ground below. The paddock was empty, the gate shut as he'd left it, and everything appeared as it should. A creamy moon glowed brightly, its light illuminating the area, showing him that no one lurked in those God-awful spooky trees running down the side of the field either.

So was someone in the house? Was that it?

Leaving the window, he walked to the door, looking back at Sarah to make sure she still slept. Her chest rose and fell, her hair spread out over the pillow, and he wanted nothing more than to get back into bed to nestle beside her. But keeping her safe was more important. Regretfully, he turned away and padded downstairs to the kitchen, picking up his discarded jeans and pulling them on. He put on his shirt, fastening the buttons as he walked over to the window, and stared out again.

No one there.

He searched the house, footsteps seeming loud in the stillness of the night, and came up empty. He returned to the kitchen, stuffing his feet into his boots then finding the key in a drawer in the sideboard. Sarah would be fine inside alone for the time it took him to search the grounds. He didn't intend being a minute longer than he had to.

Outside, after locking the door and slipping the key in his jeans pocket, he circled the house, again finding nothing. He made for the tackle barn, wondering if whoever had come visiting had holed up inside. No horses nickered in the stables nearby and he gave a small sigh of relief. They'd be the first to complain if some stranger interrupted their night. Nevertheless, nerves skittered in his belly, and he pushed the heavy door open, bracing himself for an attack. Inky darkness bled into everything, and he couldn't even make out the tool table to his right or the tackle hanging on the wall to his left. He cursed himself for not bringing a flashlight and took another step inside.

There. What was that smell?

He sniffed, long and hard, and caught an unmistakeable whiff of Clark. No wonder the horses hadn't caused a fuss. They knew Clark, were used to him. So Travis had been right. The man hadn't intended making him wait and fret for him to get back at him at all—he'd come right out fighting at the earliest opportunity.

But where was he?

He sniffed again, and another, stronger scent overrode the bastard's. Rodney Dukes? What the hell would he be doing here? Travis' mind went crazy. Had Clark brought Rodney with him so they could both take Sarah against her will? Or were they here because Clark wanted to make sure Travis was overpowered before he went through with his threats? Had Clark realised he couldn't take Travis on alone? And everyone knew Sarah had a gun in each room of her house. Maybe that was it. Clark had brought Rodney along so it would be easier to distract Sarah from shooting Clark.

Walking to his right, going by instinct because his sight was obscured by darkness, Travis made it to the tool table. He patted the many surfaces of implements on top, pleased when his hand curled around a flashlight handle. He switched the beam on, arcing it through the air so the wide swathe picked up every nook and cranny.

No one was there.

What the fuck?

That tinkle sang again, and he turned to face the doorway, lunging through it and coming to a breathless stop on the dusty track outside. Rodney's and Clark's scents were stronger here—stronger than they'd been in the barn. So did that mean they'd been out here when Travis had been collecting the flashlight? He frowned at the thought. If that was the case, why hadn't he heard them, sensed them? Why did his hearing work well one minute and not the next? Not knowing was driving him nuts, and he sniffed harder, concentrating to pick up exactly where those two men were.

A slight breeze gusted over him from ahead, bringing with it the unmistakeable smell of unwashed bodies—Rodney—and a sickly sweet aftershave unique only to Clark. Had they seen him in the barn and decided to leave? Shaking his head grimly, he clenched his jaw tight and followed the smell. It grew stronger the further he walked. Relieved that the men weren't near the house and that Sarah was safe, Travis felt comfortable following the men's trail and catching up with them, demanding to know what the fuck they'd been doing on Sarah's land.

Travis walked quite a way. Nearly at the edge of Sarah's property now, he made his way to the fence border and took a minute to rest. He leaned his arms on the fence and cocked his head. No sound but the wind and his own breathing. And not two scents now but only one. Clark's. Maybe they had parted ways along here.

Climbing over the fence, Travis buoyed himself up for a long trek into town where Clark lived. He cast his gaze all around and, finding nothing untoward, decided to strip and shift. The faster he apprehended Clark the better. He draped his clothes over the fence, butted his boots against it, and let the wolf encompass him. The shift was quick, a *pop-snap-pop* of bones that heralded his body changing shape as he became the animal Sarah suspected him to be. Down on all fours, the crisp air cooling his tongue as he panted, Travis scented the air and took off in the direction of Clark's place.

Shit, he loved this, running free, the wind in his fur, his paws pummelling the soft ground. His head usually cleared of all unsettling thoughts when he became his wolf, leaving him refreshed and ready to fight another day when he returned to being a man. Not tonight, though. No, he had Sarah's safety on his mind—and catching up with Clark to find out what the fuck the man was playing at in the middle of the goddamn night.

As the silhouettes of town houses on the horizon grew closer, Clark's scent came from another direction. Travis turned to his left, head tilted as he processed why the bastard's smell would be coming from over there. His stomach churned with realisation.

Gordon's Creek was that way.

Fuck. Fucking shit!

At full speed, Travis took off, galloping over the fields, his intent to reach that creek paramount. If Clark hadn't killed that hiker and dumped him there before, what the fuck business did he have even being at Gordon's Creek tonight? The man didn't strike Travis as the type to take a midnight dip, though God knew the jerk needed to wash the stench of that cheap aftershave off his skin.

Panting hard, Travis reached the creek and came to a stop. The mouldy smell of the water disguised Clark's aroma a little, but it was still there all the same. This section of the creek was narrow, the width the same from right over there in the distance, but about three minutes' walk to his left, the breadth widened, opening up to a deep pool that stretched on for a mile or so before it tapered again. He wasn't exactly sure where the hiker had been found or why the dead man nagged at his mind this way, but he decided to obey his instincts and follow the creek where it was still narrow. He thought he recalled mention of the hiker being on a steep bank where bushes grew thick and fast, his body hidden beneath.

The dark shapes of bushes loomed to his right, maybe two hundred metres away, and, as he turned to walk that way, he growled at his instincts being correct.

He could smell Clark stronger now.

He loped towards the bushes, the feeling creeping inside him that Clark was inside them or behind them, ready to pounce. The man had drawn him out here, he was sure of it, to kill him like he had the hiker.

Oh, fuck. Is he really capable of killing someone, though?

As he drew nearer to the bushes, Travis squinted at the odd, dark shape in front of them. What the hell *was* that? He padded closer. Caught the scent of blood. His stomach muscles clenched, and he fought back the urge to retch.

Oh, no. Please, God, no…

He walked on, steeling himself for the worst, and when he reached the mound he almost threw up. A female body rested there, naked, legs splayed, breasts hacked off. Blood spatter streaked her belly and legs, recent if the stench was anything to go by. Long hair covered the woman's face and, unable to be of much help in wolf form, Travis shifted. The change seemed to take longer than usual, but he realised that the awful slow motion of suspended time in situations like this had taken over. In his human form—absurdly conscious of standing naked beside a corpse, knowing it was inappropriate but unable to do anything about it—he sucked in a few deep breaths to calm his fast-beating heart. He hunkered down, legs wobbly, and reached out to check the woman's wrist for a pulse.

He didn't find it.

Panic set in. His teeth chattered and his throat tightened. Pausing to still his racing mind, to remember what he should do in an instance like this, he struggled to form a cohesive thought. The discovery of her, the sight of her, the smell of her had leeched all sense out of him. Touching her wrist and finding out she was dead had been the final thing to tip him over the edge.

Focus! This isn't about you. It's about this woman and finding who the fuck killed her. Clark. It was Clark… Had to be.

He took one last, huge breath then lifted her hair from her face.

Macy Jo stared back at him.

Travis sprang back, landing on his ass, a shout of surprise barking out of his mouth. What the hell? Why the fuck would Clark want to kill Macy?

"Hey! You there!" someone shouted.

Travis turned to where the voice had originated, his eyes misty with tears of shock, his heart thumping way too wildly for his liking. Two figures barrelled towards him, and, despite being naked, Travis scrambled to his feet, relief pouring into him that help had arrived.

"Fucking hell! Thank God you're here. Macy Jo. Someone killed Macy Jo. Help me, will you? You got a cell? Ring for the police." Travis looked back down at Macy, unable to comprehend the young woman's death.

"One of us *is* the police, asshole."

Clark.

Travis whipped his head around, eyes clear now. Clark came abreast of him, grabbing Travis' wrist in a harsh grip.

"What the fuck are you doing here?" Travis demanded. "And get your goddamned hands off me!" He tried to break free, but Clark held him strong. Had the shock of finding Macy rendered Travis weak? He tugged some more, ineffective in his efforts to make the guy let him go. It didn't make sense, Clark being able to constrain him like this.

"You hear that, Stephen?" Clark asked.

Travis glanced away from Clark to the other man. The bombshell of seeing Stephen here as well had Travis' mouth opening and closing with no sound coming out for a few seconds. He managed a quiet, "What the fuck?" before Clark butted in again.

"What did I tell you, Stephen? I said I saw him coming out here with no clothes on, didn't I? Fucking freak bastard." Clark winked at Travis. "And oh, Lord, there's Macy Jo, dead like that hiker last year when *he* strolled into town." He jerked his head at Travis and smirked.

Travis tried to yank his arm away, but it felt heavy, useless. He stared at Stephen, who stared back, eyes glazed, his face that of someone under the influence. Had Clark brought him up here *drunk?*

"Stephen?" Travis said. "Macy Jo is dead. I found her here just now. Don't listen to that prick!"

"But he's naked, Stephen," Clark said. "You see that? Big ole cock hanging there for all to see. Killing women in the nude. Whatever is the goddamn world coming to, I wonder?"

Travis' mind sparked, the fuzziness shifting some. "If I killed her, why aren't I covered in blood? She was hacked up, for fuck's sake. And get. Your fucking hands. Off me!" He pulled free at last, going back down on his knees beside Macy Jo, stricken by the sight of her but wanting to do something to help. He called over his shoulder, "One of you give me your fucking coat so we can cover this poor woman up."

When no coat sailed through the air towards him, Travis lost it. He jumped up, striding towards Clark, who stood his ground, that infernal smirk still in place.

"What the hell is wrong with you two? Ring for the deputy. It's clear Stephen's in no fit state to deal with this!"

Clark hawked then spat. "You hear that, Stephen? Guy here says you're a shitty sheriff. That you can't do your job. Reckon you'll be wanting to arrest him, right? I mean, we found him up here with a dead body. What the fuck is that all about, huh?"

Travis lifted one arm to throw a punch at Clark, but the other man raised his forearm to block it. Stephen came up behind Travis, yanking his arms behind him to apply cuffs.

"Oh, so you're with it now, are you?" Travis snarled, struggling so Stephen couldn't constrain him.

Clark went around the back of Travis and helped Stephen out. With Travis bound, Clark kicked him in the backs of his knees, sending Travis sprawling to the ground.

"Go and see to the body, Stephen. Do your job and call the deputy."

As Travis staggered to his feet, off balance without his arms by his sides, he watched in horror as Stephen obeyed. The sheriff knelt and brought out his notebook.

"What the fuck have you done to him, Clark? You given him something?"

Clark leaned in close. "That'd be telling, wouldn't it? Just like it'd be telling if I said the brew you've been drinking during tea breaks with us at the ranch has messed with your senses a little. Didn't feel that little prick from a needle in your arm just now either, did you?"

"You fucking asshole!"

Travis kicked out, but Clark stepped back just in time. Travis' leg kept going, the momentum sending him full circle, fucking with his balance. For the third time since he'd arrived here he was down on the ground.

The small hairs on his neck prickled.

Oh, Jesus Christ…

The shift began, his arms painful as his body tried to change in the usual way. His wrists thinned just in time, and he slid the cuffs off, bringing his hands in front of him. In a matter of seconds he stood in wolf form before Clark, baring his teeth and growling a warning.

"Holy fuck!" Clark sprang back, eyes wide, hands held up in surrender.

That's not going to work this time, asshole…

Travis leapt forward, shoving Clark to the ground.

"Stephen! Help! A fucking wolf!"

Travis put his front paws on Clark's chest and snarled. The man lay stupefied, scared shitless. If Travis was in human form he'd have laughed. He glanced at the sheriff. Stephen was in a world of his own, scribbling notes.

Jesus Christ…

He looked back down at Clark, debating whether to rip his fucking throat out like he'd promised.

"It's you, isn't it?" Clark said, narrowing his eyes. "Goddamn knew it was you outside Sarah's. How the fuck do you do that?" Clark shook his head, some of the fear disappearing from his eyes. He smiled, his fleshy lips wet and quivering. "You know what? You're wasting time here, fucker."

Travis cocked his head. *What?*

Clark's bravado returned. "Yeah. You'd better get ready to run, wolf boy. You in the mood for a sprint?"

Travis checked Clark over for signs of a gun, annoyed with himself that the human side of him prevented him from killing this motherfucker.

What the hell is he on about?

Clark lifted his arm slowly and peered at his watch. "Yeah, right about…now."

Travis dipped his head, opening his mouth to release a menacing growl.

"Aww, get the hell off me, wolf boy. You need to take a jog. Back to your clothes. You'll find the next clue there."

Travis hesitated, wondering if this was just another of Clark's sick games.

"Run along, freak." Clark laughed, holding his belly, delirious with hilarity.

Travis stared at him. Clark's switch from being so scared then laughing as though nothing fazed him was something Travis hadn't seen before. He urged himself to clamp his teeth around that throat and bite hard.

Clark stopped laughing abruptly. "You still here? Go on, fuck off. Check your clothes. You want another clue?" He paused, licking his lips. "Sarah's alone, right?"

Travis sped away, leaving that fucked-up scene behind him. He'd deal with it later when he knew

Sarah was safe. He'd call the deputy and offer up an interview. No way was he going down for a murder he didn't commit.

The air burned his lungs. His legs screamed from the vigorous exercise. His mouth dried out. Head pounding with panic, paws smacking the ground, he raced back the way he had come. It seemed to take an age for him to reach the fence where he'd left his clothes. He shifted again, tired out from the amount of times he'd changed tonight, and dived for his jeans. Searched the pockets. Searched the ground. Searched them both again.

The key to Sarah's house was gone.

A slight rustle sounded behind him, then a blinding pain entered his head. His knees buckled, and as he fell to the ground, his last thought was that someone had hit him with a goddamn baseball bat.

Chapter Ten

The following morning, Sarah blinked rapidly against the sunlight shining through the thin material of her bedroom curtains. She rolled over, the aches and pains reminding her of the adventures of the night before.

"Travis," she called, frowning when she couldn't hear him. Moving out of the bed, she pulled on her robe and looked in the bathroom, then his room and, finding them empty, went downstairs, sure he would be around somewhere.

She glanced through the kitchen window. The men worked, but Travis was nowhere to be seen.

Had he gone and left her?

Don't be ridiculous. He's out there somewhere, that's all.

The kettle wheezing was the only sound in the room. Sarah barely heard it. It felt like her heart was being ripped out as she thought the worst.

Travis was gone and not coming back.

She stood in the kitchen for the longest time, her whole body working on automatic. She didn't think about her actions. She removed the kettle from the stove, adding milk, sugar and coffee to two cups, which she then filled with boiling water. Her hands shook, and tears wet her cheeks. Until recently, she hadn't cried in an age, had vowed not to over any man, yet here she was, mind elsewhere, crying out her upset, anger and loss of a man she'd thought had given a shit about her.

How wrong could I fucking be?

She glanced down at the cups and frowned. Took one and threw it in the sink, yelling out her pain. Sarah held on to the sink and raged, the painful noises coming out of her revealing her heartbreak. The first time she'd opened her heart and body to a man and he was gone.

A knock at her back door made Sarah stand and gather her wits. She hastily wiped her face, took a deep breath, went to the door and opened it.

"How can I help you, Gavin?" Her voice was calm, if a little hoarse, and she knew her face must be red.

Gavin stepped over the threshold. "Sorry, Miss French, but the men and I heard ya screaming and we were worried." He pulled his Stetson from his head and fiddled with the damn thing.

She shouldn't be listening to his worry, even though it touched her somewhere deep inside that the men cared enough to check on her. She shouldn't even have to deal with this shit. Did they care she was upset just because she was a woman? If she was a man, would one of them have walked up to her damn house and asked if she was okay? No, she didn't think they would.

Not caring about her naked state underneath her robe, she placed her hands on his chest, gently pushed him out of her house and down the steps. The men, some of them old workers from when her father was in charge, glanced at her with pity in their eyes.

She didn't want or need their pity—she was fine on her own like she always had been, and she wouldn't have any of these men tell her otherwise. They'd probably heard all about the fracas at Macy Jo's last night. Maybe guessed Travis had brought her home, fucked her, then fucked off.

"Have you got a problem?" she yelled.

They all stared at the ground or kept their gazes everywhere else but on her.

She was done with this shit.

"I asked you guys a question!" Sarah was determined to have the fight that was brewing inside her. She knew she shouldn't be taking it out on the men, but Travis wasn't here, and if he ever turned up again, she'd have lost the urge to yell and scream at him.

"We were just worried about you, Sarah. The men mean nothing by it," one of the ranch workers spoke up.

"I don't need any of your worry. I don't need anything from you except work. Take a good old look at me. I'll let you know exactly what's wrong before the gossip-mongers really get going. That way you'll have heard it directly from me and not some nasty old bitch in town. I'm a fallen woman. I gave my body to Travis Williams last night and he fucked off."

Her outburst was a little too dramatic, but she hadn't been able to stop herself. The tears were fast flowing again, her anger rife. She shook from the pent-up emotion dying to be unleashed—and, God, there was so much more inside her to come out. She didn't want to do it now, or here, but she knew she wouldn't see Travis in time to let it loose.

"No lady like you should be talking like that."

Her eyes blurred against the waves of pain at the unseen man's words. She was a lady, her daddy had told her that. She'd given her heart and body to Travis thinking he'd meant what he'd said, and now he wasn't here, just like her damn instincts had screamed. Was this normal protocol for guys to lie in order to get a fuck? In truth, she didn't have the first clue what to expect, not with guys like that anyway, but she'd hoped it would have been something special. Thought *he* had been someone special.

This was what you got for giving your heart to a man? Crushed, humiliated and alone? She should have just stuck with her old life, keeping everyone at a distance. She didn't need men then and she wouldn't need them now. In fact, she was already sick of seeing fucking men.

"Get the fuck off my ranch," she screamed at the workers.

They looked at her, shocked, and in that moment she couldn't have cared less.

"You heard me. Get the fuck off my ranch and don't come back."

She threw a stone off her porch. It landed somewhere in the middle of the group, kicking up dust. The crowd dispersed slowly, the older ones glancing at her with sadness clearly written in their eyes.

Panting for breath, she stalked back into her kitchen, knowing she'd really messed things up now. With no men to help run the ranch it'd go to ruin, but a part of her revelled in not caring. They were out of a job, no wages coming in from here on out, and she was to blame. Her and her hot temper.

But her stubborn pride wouldn't allow her to call them back.

She shut the back door. It rattled inside the frame. She looked at the door Travis had spent so long repairing. He'd done a really good job. Running her hand along the wood, such a simple touch, she thought she could feel Travis. It was a bizarre and surreal moment. She sensed fresh air and panic as he ran, as though she was tied to him somehow. Her fuzzy brain was connecting with something… Was that a wolf she saw in her mind's eye? Shaking her head against the craziness, she ploughed her fist through one of the small window panes in the door.

She cried out with the pain but at the same time relished it. The pain was a welcome relief from all the hurtful emotions in her heart.

Shaking her head to try to disperse the thought of Travis and a wolf, she pulled her hand back inside and wrapped her fist in a towel. She would have to go to the emergency room. Hadn't her daddy told her to control her temper otherwise it would start to cost money?

"Sorry, Daddy, but I'm sure this once you can forgive me," she whispered and made her way upstairs to dress.

Once inside her room, she stared at the bed she'd shared with Travis, where she'd lost her precious virginity and given Travis more of herself than she'd ever given another human being. Tying the cloth into a knot on her bloodied knuckles, she pulled the duvet from the bed and threw it in the corner by the door. She continued to strip the bed, cheeks blazing hot at the red stain on her sheets, until it was bare and she was panting and sweaty from her work.

"That's it, I quit. I'm selling this place, Daddy. Do you hear me? I want fuck all to do with this shithole." She screamed, cursed and pushed all of her passion into her anger.

Still sweating, determined to get done with everything, she changed into baggy sweat pants and shirt, intent on keeping her mind focused. She would rid her life of her problems. Go to the emergency room, get herself checked out, and then she'd put this place up for sale. Screw the town and Macy Jo and all the Travises of this world. She was done. One guy and that was enough for her.

Once fully dressed, she pulled her hair into a pony tail, washed her face and the excess blood off her hand, wincing at the sting. She retied it with the cloth and gazed at her reflection in the small bathroom mirror, unable to see much beyond a huge pair of empty eyes looking back at her. Not satisfied, she went to the full-length mirror in her father's bedroom. She took time to look at herself. Even in the baggy clothes she could see the outline of her every curve. Should she feel different, or *did* she look different from last night? She stared harder, trying to detect any subtle difference about her person. Her ass was still a little too big and her breasts fuller than the average woman's. And her eyes still shot daggers.

She could see the swell of her hips, see Travis' hand glide down and hold them. See Travis standing behind her. He wasn't there, but her mind remembered him and wanted him. Her body responded with the budding of her nipples, jutting against her shirt, as well as a rapid pulse in her pussy. She cupped her mound through the restricting fabric and moaned. He'd awakened her as a woman, and, as much as she cursed and scolded men and her life, she knew she would never be the same. Her body was alive and ready for her man. Her nipples were sore from his suckling last night and her pussy ached from the use and the need to be fucked.

All of these changes were part of who she was and, no matter how much she raved or was driven crazy, this was who she was.

Her mind and sanity returning, she stopped the self-torment, knowing she was being stupid. Taking a deep breath, she decided she would go to the hospital then make calls to all of the men who worked for her.

She owed them an apology.

What if Travis has only gone into town?

What if he'd got called away for something? Now she had a calmer attitude, she saw a multitude of '*What if…?*' questions forming that he could answer if she found him innocently shopping for new leather oil or visiting the blacksmith—and that could be a possibility.

"Bad, Sarah, very bad."

She remembered the other spare key, which she'd left for him on the hook of a ceramic key holder, shaped like a pig, she had in the hallway. Had she even told him he could use it, that it was there? She wasn't sure and left her father's bedroom, gathered up the dirty laundry from hers and put it in the machine downstairs, then made herself a coffee. She walked slowly to the hallway in search of that spare key. If it was hanging on its little hook, she'd know Travis wasn't coming back, but if it wasn't there then she had some serious work to do to make it up to the men.

How she could repay them for being such a bitch?

Closing her eyes for the last final steps, nerves got the better of her and she stood holding on to the unit that lived there.

"Open your eyes, Sarah," she said.

She ignored herself.

"Come on, this is ridiculous. Open your eyes." She opened them and her joy when the spare key was gone overwhelmed her. She squealed in happiness and jumped. Travis hadn't abandoned her. There was no key. Shaking with relief, she started making breakfast for herself, whistling.

She wondered if she had enough cash to throw the men a disco or something with a band. Anything they wanted by way of an apology.

The phone rang, and she removed her eggy bread from the stove and went to the living room where one of the only phones lay.

"Hello," she answered.

Maybe it was Travis?

There was a pause on the other end.

"Hello?" she said again.

"Is this Sarah French?"

She didn't recognise the voice. "Yes, who's calling?"

"It's John, John Baines… Macy Jo's husband?"

Wow, on the phone he sounded normal, nothing like the terrifying man he'd been previously.

"What's the matter, John?" Sarah still recalled how Macy hadn't come to her aid last night and how it had hurt. Out of all the townsfolk, Sarah had been sure Macy would have been on her side. They'd been really good friends growing up, and Sarah had attended their wedding.

"Is Macy with you?"

Sarah frowned. "No, why? She was at the bar last night when a lot of shit went down. She rang you. Didn't you go and help her out?" She straightened a picture, wondering what on earth was going on.

"I couldn't make it. Babysitter issues. I phoned everyone I know last night. Shit, I even went knocking on neighbours' doors to take the kids for an hour or two. Fucking nothing."

Frustration bled from his voice, and she couldn't help but think, if he'd been nicer, he'd have had no problem finding help with the little ones. She wouldn't say it, though. John was like Clark, his temper unpredictable and volcanic when it started, and she didn't have the head to deal with him right now.

"Look, John, I'm busy. What is this about?"

A pause ensued before he continued.

"Macy Jo didn't come home last night."

"What? Is that normal?"

"Yes."

Sarah was confused. "What, it's normal that your wife doesn't come home after locking up the bar?"

"She sometimes stays there if she's worked too late."

"Have you phoned the bar? Maybe she slept over again or something?" she suggested.

"I've phoned. No one's seen or heard from her. She left the bar, I know that, but she hasn't come home. I thought she'd have gone to you to apologise about what happened. I heard she stayed quiet when Clark upset you."

This morning was getting weirder and weirder.

Sarah was about to suggest he call the sheriff when a noise from the dining room stopped her. "Hold on, John, I think I heard something."

She carried the phone by her side, heard him shouting her name down the line. He sounded panicked. She didn't understand why—nothing bad ever happened around here. Macy Jo had probably stopped by somewhere overnight to get away from the crap that had happened. Who knew? Maybe she was pissed off at John for not going to the bar after she'd called him.

Sarah walked past the hallway into the dining room and stopped, catching something in her peripheral. She took a step back and looked at her open front door.

She heard John panting down the line and lifted the phone to her ear.

"What do you think happened to Macy Jo?" she whispered, walking to her door.

"Please, Sarah, please tell me she's there."

She opened the door a little more. There was nothing there. Sunlight lit the hills and valleys, but she couldn't make anything bad out. Frowning, she shut the door, heart tripping.

"Sarah? Sarah?"

"I'm here, John."

"Why are you whispering?"

He sounded worried, and Sarah couldn't begin to describe the pounding in her chest or the panic taking over. Something was wrong.

"I think someone is in my house, John," she admitted, moving her back to the wall. She peeked round the corner and glanced into the sitting room. She was sure she was losing her mind, but she couldn't stop the fear snaking through her.

"Get the fuck out of there, Sarah. You fucking stupid?" John growled.

Usually, she'd have taken extreme offence at his talk, but right now she completely agreed with him. Like in the movies where she screamed for the silly bitch to run for her life, Sarah did the opposite and checked the rooms in her house.

"Please, phone someone, anyone, John. I'm keeping the line free in case I need to call the sheriff." She cancelled the call and hugged the device to her chest. "Just so you know," she called out like a mad woman, "I have a gun in every room!" Great, every other woman ran for their lives and she was here threatening the guy—without even picking up one of the guns she was threatening him with. What the hell was wrong with her? "Travis? Is that you?"

She walked to the kitchen and ran to the cooker. It was burning a towel on the hob. She switched the cooker off and turned, pressing her back to the oven. It was clear now, someone was here. She hadn't left that damn towel there. She looked around the room, seeking any clue as to the intruder's whereabouts. She cursed the house for being old and having so many different places for a person to hide. Cursed her damn self for not reaching into the sideboard to fetch the gun there.

She strode forward to get it out, but a heart necklace dangling from one of the hooks on the wall diverted her attention. She took it down and looked at it, not recognising the piece. It wasn't one of hers. It was a locket, and she opened the latch. Macy Jo and John stared back from the small pictures placed in each side. One big black cross was drawn on Macy Jo's face, and Sarah knew where the necklace had come from.

The scream in her throat got stuck and fear came suddenly and with full force. She had to get out of here—now. She dropped the necklace and the phone and ran to the back door. She pulled on the handle but the door wouldn't budge, and her hand was now bleeding through the cloth from the window cut she'd got earlier.

Crying out, shaking her head at her stupidity in dropping the phone—had fear sent her dumb?—she ran for the front door and stopped when she saw the spare key in the lock. She'd painted the tip with some pink nail varnish so she knew which one was the main key and which was the spare.

Sarah stared at the key, terrified by what it meant. Travis should have that key. Was he and Macy both being missing significant? No, it couldn't be possible. She knew Travis, didn't she?

She backed away, shaking her head again, not knowing what to do. Her back hit a wall of hard muscle. A hand went over her mouth, covering her scream, while another bound her hands at her sides, holding her steady.

She tried to scream again but no sound escaped, the noise muffled by the meaty palm.

"Now, you're a wee little thing, aren't you? I can see what Clark likes about you. A fighter he wants to tame."

The stench of bad breath and unkempt male assailed her nostrils and she almost passed out.

"I wonder what he'll do to you first."

The disgusting bastard behind her was revolting.

"What did it? The necklace or the key? What scared you the most, little darlin'?"

She recognised that voice. She knew his smell and panic set in further. His hand relented for enough time for her to let a scream out.

He dragged her out of the hallway, and Sarah bit down and kicked, lashing out as much as possible.

The phone rang in the background, and she heard John screaming her name in her mind.

Macy Jo was gone and she wasn't coming back—Sarah knew that as well as she knew her own name.

They'd all mistaken Clark for being the bad guy around these parts, but it was Rodney damn Dukes.

He laughed at her struggle, but she finally got free, running into the kitchen. She gripped a cup, threw it at him, then rushed for the back door. He was bigger, taller and faster. He grabbed her arms and threw her into the wall with enough force that her head slammed against it. She collapsed in a heap on the floor, tried to get away again but couldn't move fast enough. She fought him as hard and as fast as she could, but he yanked her hair, dragging her back, then rubbed his crotch against her ass, making her retch.

"Get the fuck off me, you asshole!" she yelled.

"We're going to enjoy you, little darlin'. Let's see if your wolf boy will want you when we're through with you."

A cloth covered her mouth and, eyes wide with fear, Sarah fought the darkness for as long as possible. The throb in her hand eased. She looked at her hand, the cloth gone now, saw the cuts from the glass and the dripping blood through glazed eyes. She tried to gaze around the room, but her senses were dulling. She felt a few droplets of blood drip off her skin. Her head grew thick, mind syrupy.

He released her hair, and she fell sideways, letting the darkness claim her.

Chapter Eleven

Travis awoke but kept his eyes closed. He had a blinding headache and reached up a tentative hand to feel the sore spot on the back of his skull. He winced at a fresh slice of pain. His hair was hard, as though something sticky had dried on it. Something tickled his arm, and it felt suspiciously like…grass?

What the fuck?

He snapped his eyes open, realising several things at once—he was outside, under some bush or other, and he was fucking freezing. As though his acknowledging the cold gave his body permission to react, goosebumps spread out over his skin, and his teeth chattered. He looked at his hand. Dark red specks decorated his fingertips. Dried blood?

He crawled out from under the bush on hands and knees, remembering why he was here. Last night. Finding Macy Jo. Clark and Stephen appearing. Running to the fence, trying to find Sarah's key. Being struck and blacking out. He sat on the grass—damn cold on his bare ass—his clothes and the fence nowhere in sight.

So he'd been moved from the spot where he'd been hit, then.

Grimacing from the pain in his throbbing head, he stood, his mind immediately going to Sarah. He could only hope that the key was lost, had fallen out of his pocket and nestled in the grass, and hadn't been taken. He could only hope she was safe.

What time was it? The men on her ranch started early, almost when the cock crowed, so she wouldn't have been on her own for long, not really. He'd left her about...what, two in the morning to investigate the noises?

He glanced at the sky and, judging by the placement of the sun, it was around ten. He hadn't slept this late in years. He hadn't intended on leaving Sarah by herself for eight hours either.

Clark's revelation came back to him, barrelling into his mind, spreading like a rancid, bitter acid.

'That'd be telling, wouldn't it? Just like it'd be telling if I said the brew you've been drinking during tea breaks with us at the ranch has messed with your senses a little.'

What the fuck had been in it? Whoever had hit him last night—had they given him more when he was out for the damn count?

He decided to shift—better to be a wolf than a naked man—and run home then call Sarah to make sure she was okay. If he turned up at the ranch as a wolf he'd be shot without a doubt, and if he arrived naked they might not let him near her home anyway, no matter what he told them. They were fiercely protective of her, if only she'd stop and see it.

His need to reach her quickly caught hold of him, and he concentrated, shifting, the pain in his head vanishing.

Low voices came from his right, startling him a little. He backed into the bushes, spiteful thorns snagging his coat, and waited for whomever it was to pass by. From the looks of the field opposite, he was on the outskirts of Sarah's land. Mountains lay ahead—those in the region of Gordon's Creek if he wasn't mistaken. He shuddered at the memory of being there, of what he'd seen.

What the hell are people doing this far out here?

Maybe a horse had bolted, he didn't know, but he *did* know it was unusual for anyone to be taking a walk or working this far out. These fields were used for pasture when the grass in the ones closest to the ranch had been bitten down to the ground. He narrowed his eyes to see into the distance to his far left. No black dots scattered about. Why weren't the horses grazing out there?

The voices grew louder, although they weren't raised to anything above a low murmur. Two men, their identities indecipherable. Travis strained his ears for a clue. One came with the hoarse cackle of a laugh that chilled his bones and made the hairs on his neck stand up.

Fucking Clark.

What the hell had been the deal with him last night anyway? Travis knew Clark was a dirty son of a bitch, but to try to get him framed for murder? The bastard must want Sarah to himself real bad. And did that mean the deputy would be looking for Travis now? Why hadn't the one who'd whacked him around the head told the police where he was? Why had he even *been* whacked when he'd left Clark at Gordon's Creek? Who else wanted him harmed?

"He should be asleep for a little while yet," Clark said. "The amount you gave him was too much, dipshit. I told you only five mils. I already gave him a jab at the creek. We need him alive if he's gonna take the rap."

So Clark still intended for Travis to take the blame for Macy Jo's death. Fucking great. People around here were so small-minded, Travis would be banged up and judged before it ever got to court. He'd go down for a crime he hadn't committed, the judge and jury too afraid of Clark to go against him and give Travis a fair trial.

"Sorry," the other man said.

Rodney Dukes.

Motherfucker!

Travis stopped a growl escaping and peered through the foliage. There they were, coming towards the bush, walking as though they didn't have a care in the damn world, like they were out on a stroll, nothing better to do with their time. How the hell did they sleep at night? Didn't they have consciences? It looked as if they'd both taken time to shower, dress in clean clothes, and they'd even brushed their hats by the looks of them. Another day—another normal day to them.

Jesus Christ!

"She tied up nice and tight?" Clark asked, chewing on a matchstick, one hand grabbing his crotch.

Sarah? If they've fucking hurt her...

Travis wanted to spring out of his hiding place and attack them, but he couldn't risk them drawing their guns. If they injured him—or, worse, killed him—he'd be no good to Sarah anyway.

"Yeah. You sure you want a piece of her?" Rodney coughed. "I mean, she's not right clever. Had a phone on her at one point when I went to collect her but put it down. Doesn't strike me as a woman with all her farcults in place."

"Farcults? What the fucking hell are you going on about, asshole?" Clark stopped walking and stared at Rodney as though he wanted to land one on him.

Rodney stopped too, a frown firmly in place. "You know, she ain't got all her marbles."

"Faculties. You mean faculties. Jeez, man, you're a fine one to talk. And so what if she hasn't got all her *farcults?* Who needs a woman with brains when you're just fucking her hole?"

Rodney laughed, and they resumed walking.

"Oh, yeah," Clark said. "I want a piece of that, sure as fucking shit I do. So, she's secure, right?"

"Yeah, yeah. Tied her with them thick-ass ropes you got out of her own damn tackle shed." Rodney whooped and slapped his thigh.

The sound sickened Travis, and so did the sight of them as they came closer. They stopped right in front of the bush, their boot fronts wet with dew, same as the hems of their jeans.

"You sure you left him here?" Clark asked, narrowing his eyes as he scanned the ground left to right.

"Yeah, right here." Rodney frowned and scratched his head. "Well, I'll be damned if he didn't get up and walk away."

"Shit! Fucking shit!" Clark stomped one foot.

"Hey, boss. Doesn't matter. Deputy'll have him. Stephen will see to that. Suits us, right?" Rodney gave Clark a hopeful look.

"No, it doesn't. I wanted him free for what I have in mind for Sarah. I need Travis being on the loose to prove that when he's got a mind he goes off killing women. And I wanted to give the fucker a beating first, humiliating me at Macy Jo's like that." Clark smoothed his hands over his face, as though the action would keep him calm.

Rodney's face took on a dreamy look. "Fine piece of ass Macy was, too."

"Yeah." Clark stared into the distance, fiddling with his fly. "She fitted around my cock just right, tasted well and good last night, too. Shame she had to go really—I wouldn't have minded a revisit. I love a woman who struggles. Made out she didn't want my dick, but she wanted it all right. They all do."

Travis bared his teeth. Clark clearly had no remorse for taking a mother away from her children, a wife from her husband, a good woman and friend from a community. All she was to him was a means to an end, someone to be discarded once she'd served her purpose. What a waste of a life.

"You hate Travis that much?" Rodney sounded genuinely confused.

You and me both, asshole.

"Yeah, bastard has the woman I want, the job I want. You know why it was so easy for you to take her this morning, don't you?"

Rodney shook his head. "Nope. I just reckoned the men were out buying horses—she'd been saying she was gonna get some more."

"She does the buying herself, doesn't trust the likes of us. No, she fired the damn lot of them. Came right out and told them all that Travis had fucked her and left her, then told them to leave. Big buzz about it in town. But then you won't have heard about it, being with Sarah and all. Being as dim as you are. I tell you, God helps those who help themselves, and he knew I was about to help myself to her tasty little cunt, so he made the way a bit easier." Clark laughed, and it sounded broken, raspy and phlegm-filled.

He hawked and spat—the man's infuriating habit churning Travis' gut. The mucus landed on the grass beside Clark's boot.

Travis panted, short, quick breaths. He was getting angrier by the goddamn second. He wanted to run, to get Sarah from wherever the hell she was, and then sort Clark out once and for all.

"So," Clark said, more sombre now. "We have a slight change of plan. Travis has gone. Might have fucked off out of town or might stay around to cause us a bit of shit. Either way, we need to get back to that bitch. She's got some cock to suck, farcults or no farcults. Jesus, I'm getting hard just thinking about it."

"Can I watch this time, boss?"

"No, you fucking can't!"

Rodney sighed. "Well, then. Let's just check a bit further along first. It was dark when I clocked him one. I might have got the location wrong."

"Wouldn't surprise me."

Their boots moved, went out of sight. Travis counted to thirty before slinking out of the bushes and running full tilt the way Clark and Rodney had come. Their scent still lingered, and, despite him feeling a little groggy from the after effects of whatever the hell they'd given him, he reckoned he'd be able to pick their smell up until it led him to where Sarah was.

Anger fuelled his speed. What right did they have to take her like that? And did Clark have plans to dispose of her the same way he had with Macy Jo once he'd finished with her?

Fucking asshole.

Their scent faded a little but was definitely still there, a faint wisp of their usual aromas spiced with whatever they'd bathed with. He lost track for a second and stopped abruptly, lifting his nose to the sky. There—straight ahead. Travis ran again, heading for his own home.

What the hell? They've damn well taken her to my place so there's no disputing it's me who took her?

He didn't question his instincts, just kept going, the men's scents fading more now, overridden by Sarah's—and the unmistakeable tang of fear. Hers or his own, he didn't know. He leapt over the fence separating Sarah's land from that which his cottage stood on and pounded towards the small dwelling. He smelt her around him and came to a halt, eyeing his surroundings then his home. There were no signs of a break-in—his dark oak front door was closed tight, his white sash window frames unmarred by a tyre iron or whatever the fuck people broke in with these days. He padded around back—no evidence of foul play there, either.

Confused, he cocked his head and listened hard, staring at the large barn that housed his truck.

The barn!

He ran then, right for it at immense speed, and reached the double, slatted wood doors in record time. They were locked—a shiny new chain had been wound around the crescent-shaped silver handles and a polished brass padlock held it in place. He pressed his nose to a slight gap between two slats and breathed deep. Sarah's scent filled his nose, strong, so heavenly, and it was *her* fear he'd detected. He scooted around so he could peer through the slats with one eye, conscious that Clark and Rodney might be back all too soon, although he'd bet they'd be a while as neither of them could run like a damn wolf. Still, he'd better be cautious. Who knew if they had some other sick bastard in on their plan?

With that thought, he sniffed again. No, he only scented Sarah and the faint residue of Rodney.

The barn was dark inside, only shadowy shapes visible, no vibrant red truck or his shiny tools or work bench in perfect sight. His gaze darted from shape to shape, and he noted nothing out of the ordinary. Yet Sarah was inside, he'd bet his life on it. He reared back and made his way to the window. It was dusty, but maybe he'd get a better view there. Up on his hind legs, front paws resting on the rough, splinter-infested ledge, he stared through. Nope, no better view at all.

Fuck!

He circled the barn, spotting a loose slat around back, slanted in a drunken way. Pushing against it with his rump, he was pleased to hear it snap from his weight, giving him enough room to squeeze inside. He blinked to become accustomed to the change in light, and after a few seconds made out his truck radiator in front of him, the headlights staring out as though they belonged to a monster who watched him with dulled eyes.

He opened his mouth to call her name, forgetting for a second that he was a wolf, cursing himself for not shifting when he'd got here so he could have gone into his cottage as a man to get something he could smack the barn door with. He'd been too intent on getting inside—getting to Sarah.

A whimper left his mouth in place of her name, and Sarah answered with one of her own. He homed in on where her voice had come from and walked down the side of his truck, nose to the air, ears tuned for the slightest of sounds.

One came, a whisper of movement from the flatbed of his truck, and then another muffled whimper. The son of a bitch had tied her up in there? Quickly, he jumped into the back, landing as close to the tailgate as he could. He strained his eyes in the darkness, his sight no more use than it was when he was in human form—damn those drugs—but he saw her shape. She was huddled with her back against the cab, and he could just make out her bent legs and the coils of rope around her middle, pinning her arms to her sides.

Oh, my beautiful Sarah. What has he done to you?

He lunged forward, intent on being close to her, comforting her.

She screamed—screamed loud and long, the sound ear-splitting. He howled with her, nudging her face with his muzzle. She wriggled to get away, her scream inaudible now, even though her mouth was stretched wide, a black hole in the gloom.

It's all right, I'm here now.

She bucked, jerked, unfurled her legs and kicked out. Her foot caught his hind paws, and he lost his balance, smacking on to the truck bed and landing on his left flank. He scrabbled to stand, to go to her again, watching her as that black hole in her face disappeared and her teeth, a faint row of light grey, took its place.

"Get. The fuck. Away from me," she said, voice stern but with a slight tremor. "I've been taken out of my goddamn house, tied up, touched up, and now I'm meant to cope with a fucking *wolf*? Jesus Christ, God, give me a fucking break, will you?"

Travis swallowed, took a few steps backward. There was nothing for it but to reveal to her who he really was. If he had any chance of saving her, he'd have to do it as a man. They had little time to play with, and once he had her safely in his cottage he could get some clothes on and call the deputy so she could report her abduction.

He took a deep breath through his nostrils and closed his eyes. As he shifted, he thought, *Please don't let her freak. Please let her understand. Let her still want me.*

As his paws became hands and feet, the grit from the flatbed digging into his skin, his knees, he swallowed again and opened his eyes. Sarah stared back at him, and he didn't need light to know she looked at him with horror. Jesus Christ, he'd had no choice but to shift. She needed getting out of here. Whatever she felt for him now didn't matter, so long as she was safe.

But it *did* matter, and he'd lick his wounds later, when all this shit was cleared up and life had returned to normal.

"Travis?" she whispered. "*Travis?*"

"Yes, honey, it's me."

In true Sarah French form, and despite her always seeing things in black and white, with no room for even considering the fact that shifters existed, she shouted, "Where the *fuck* have you been?"

Chapter Twelve

Sarah couldn't believe what had happened to her in the last twenty-four hours. She'd lost her virginity, fallen in love, been abandoned then kidnapped from her own home. Been touched in places by hands she never wanted to remember. Then a wolf—a very pretty grey wolf but a wolf nonetheless—had been sniffing around her, and a naked Travis had appeared. Travis Williams, the man who'd taken her body and stolen her heart, was a goddamn wolf?

Don't digress, Sarah, think, think.

Travis Williams was a fucking wolf! She'd slept with a wolf—no, not a wolf but a man who could turn into one. What would have happened if she hadn't been on the pill and had got pregnant? Would she have given birth to a litter of baby wolves?

Okay, what the hell am I thinking?

In order to get out of this mess she'd need all of her brain cells concentrating on getting her away from here.

"I said, where the fuck have you been?" Out of everything she could have asked and said, she'd decided to shout that at him. *Typical, you'll be lucky if the guy sticks around now he's back.*

"Are you all right?" he whispered.

Did she fucking look all right? This day was getting crazier by the minute. She wanted to get the hell away from here, shoot Rodney through his thick head and cut off Clark's balls and feed them to him. How dare they take her from her own house! Lying, conniving bastards.

"I need you to be quiet and stop moving," Travis said.

What?

"I'm still tied, Travis. Do you seriously think I can make any more noise or move much beyond this crappy little space?"

"You're yelling, sweetheart, and they may come back."

Sarah could tell he was nervous, but what was he nervous about? Clark and Rodney were as thick as two barn doors. There was no way those two could do any serious damage, was there?

"Stop fretting," she snapped. "My God, Clark and Rodney have probably gone to Macy Jo's for an early drink and forgot about me. Now just get the knot, please. I can't feel parts of my body and I seriously need to pee."

He found the knot and started to undo it but stopped suddenly and looked at her. Despite the gloom, she could see the concern on his face.

"Shh! Someone's coming. I have to hide. But you'll be okay, I'll see to that. Trust me."

He jumped off the truck bed and went out of sight.

"Travis?" she whispered.

Seconds later, after a jangling of chains, Clark walked into the barn. Whose barn was she in anyway?

"Ah, my sleeping beauty is awake."

Shit, maybe she should have faked sleeping?

"What game are you playing, Clark? This one is not funny." Sarah kept her attention on him. She didn't want to alert him to Travis. Even if the guy could turn into a wolf, she didn't want anything bad to happen to him.

"I'm not playing at nothing much—yet. I'm just looking for Travis. Have you seen him?"

He came closer, climbed into the truck bed, and Sarah resisted the urge to shuffle back closer to the cab. The creep had some body odour issues along with his rank aftershave and she wasn't in the mood to play nice. He had her tied up and wasn't doing a thing about letting her go.

That pissed her off.

"Why would I have seen Travis? I slept with him last night, but this morning he was gone. What more do you want me to say?"

He smiled, showing all of his teeth, some of them rotting. He should be in a lot of pain. Why was she thinking about his teeth? She must be in some sort of shock. Why else would her mind keep moving from the fact that she was tied up in a barn and in serious danger?

"Do me a favour and untie this rope," she ordered, hoping her bossy attitude would do the trick. "I don't know what kind of sick game you're playing, but I want to go home." *And have a long steaming bath and scrub every part of me with soap.*

He reached his hand out, but instead of going for the rope he ran his fingers through her hair. He was touching her hair!

Don't move, don't flinch…

His stench reached her and she gagged, pulling away.

She started to feel scared when he laughed at her reaction. This guy was one sick puppy.

"Who was on the phone this morning?" he asked, sitting on his haunches.

"What?"

"You heard. Who called you this morning?"

Lie!

"I think it was some crank call. Why would you want to know?" She looked past him to see Rodney enter the barn, his silhouette creepy from the daylight behind him.

"I can't find him anywhere, boss."

Now she was in trouble.

"Typical limey bastard," Clark said. "Probably turned into a wolf and ran for his life."

Clark dug in his pocket and took something out. He reached a hand towards her, and a stabbing pain shot into her arm.

"What the fuck?" she yelled.

"Just a little something," Clark said. "In a while you'll feel more inclined to suck my cock."

She shuddered at the thought of it and pushed the images away. He got up and climbed out of the truck, giving Sarah time to have a quick look around, the sore spot on her arm aching. What the hell had he injected her with?

"What do you want me to do?" Rodney asked.

So Clark was the one really in charge—why did that not surprise her?

"Well, you could stand there and pretend to look pretty, dickwad." A pause. "Oh, for fuck's sake, Dukes! We continue on with the plan. Travis needs to be here and I want him. Find some way of tracking the bastard..."

They moved out of the barn and within seconds Travis appeared beside the truck.

"I'm so sorry I got you into this mess," he whispered, eyeing the barn doorway. "Close your eyes, honey."

Sarah just stared at him. This was way more than she could have ever imagined. This was not some kid game. This was serious.

"Tell me what's going on," she whispered, refusing to close her eyes.

"I need to get you out of here."

"I don't care about that right now. Just tell me what is going on. I need to know, deserve to know why you weren't there when I woke up this morning. I gave you everything, Travis, and you lied to me about the wolf thing. Tell me what the fuck is going on and what I've done to be involved." Sarah was at the end of her tether. She was fed up and angry and now that she'd accepted something bad was going on—knowing it in her gut as well as seeing it with her own eyes—Travis was going to tell her, give her some fucking answers.

She'd been tied up for the last few hours, why not a little longer?

"Now isn't the time, honey..."

"Just spit it out!"

"I'm a wolf—"

"No shit, Sherlock. I want answers to everything else—I got the wolf thing when you turned. Now stop treating me like delicate china and tell me what's going on." The tears were close. She was starting to understand some of the shit she was in and she didn't like it. Her heart was racing, her mind running faster than before. She only had half the answers to the problem and she couldn't put the pieces together unless someone told her the whole truth. Why couldn't she just be on her ranch sipping coffee and eating her boiled eggs and soldiers? She was hungry and cranky.

"Who was on the phone this morning?" he asked, still looking at the doorway.

"You as well? For God's sake, why is it so important?"

"Why do you insist on blocking me when I'm trying to help? Why do you need to know answers now—answers that can wait until later? I'm telling you, this isn't a game—"

"I realise that but—"

"But nothing! Please, baby, just tell me."

"It was John Baines, all right? Macy didn't make it home last night and he thought she might have come to my place to apologise." Why was it such a big deal?

"Well, at least we know he isn't in on it with Clark and Rodney."

"In on what? Macy going missing? John adores Macy and always has. He'd ruin anyone who hurt her. What the hell is going on? Why is everyone talking in riddles?" The rope hurt—it was too tight—and now all the questions. She needed to get out. It was too much. She couldn't breathe.

"Get me out of this rope," she begged, moving her arms and trying to stretch them out. "I need out."

She was used to the space of her ranch, to riding her horses and being free. She wasn't supposed to be tied down.

Everything was happening too fast, and not being in control had started to freak her the fuck out. When she'd been asking Travis questions, she'd felt better, but now, with him knowing more of the puzzle than she did, she was out of her depth. For the first time, she realised she *had* to see things in shades of grey—just like the many hues in Travis' wolf coat…

"Calm down, Sarah, calm down." He looked to the side through the doorway again, keeping an eye out for those two bastards, trying to keep her safe, but she no longer cared. She had to be free.

She tried to get calm, closing her eyes and taking deep breaths. It wasn't working. She had to be free—and now! She opened her eyes. Travis was gone.

Out of nowhere, a claw sliced through the rope and a wolf's mouth gently clamped on her arm, pulling her free. Sarah wrapped her arms around the animal and held him. She needed the contact, the love and everything he was willing to offer—even if he was a ball of goddamn fluff at the moment.

Her body ached and her heart ached more. She held him, placed her face into the curve of his neck and inhaled his delicious scent, evident even now. He smelt like fresh air and safety.

In her arms, he changed again.

"I've got you, honey. I've got you."

He stroked her hair, and she had never felt so safe while still in danger. He touched parts of her she'd never given to anyone, and to have him here meant more to her than anything else.

"Don't let me go, Travis. Please, don't let me go," she begged quietly, tears falling. Never before in all of her life had she pleaded with anyone, not even her father, and here she was begging a man who seemed to get her more than any other person. This wasn't a weakness—this was accepting she couldn't do this alone.

She needed Travis in her life, and waking up alone this morning had shown her how much she'd love a permanent deal with him. It scared the living hell out of her, but it was what she wanted and she wasn't prepared to give it up anymore.

Sarah understood what her daddy had meant now. She was so pleased she'd waited and given herself to a man whom she did want to be a part of her life for good.

"I need you to be Sarah right now—the strong, stubborn one. I can't have you break down on me."

He was terrified, she could sense how scared he was, yet he wasn't scared for himself but for her. She nodded and he wiped the tears from her cheeks. She had more sense than this—she wouldn't lose it now, she couldn't afford to, even if all she wanted to do was wrap her legs around his body and let him make it all better. She'd never run from a fight but right now she would gladly sink into the heat of him and hide. This was more than anything she'd ever faced. Now wasn't the time to be a bubble-blowing baby or an emotional wreck of a woman. She needed the good sense her father had graced her with.

"I'm sorry. I'm here." She moved out of his lap and tried to compose her mind. Everything seemed to be closing in on her all at once. The death of her mother and father, the troubles at the ranch, Clark and Travis…

Her mind raced with drawn-out images and she couldn't cope.

Sarah sank her fingers into her hair, shaking as pain upon pain consumed her. She couldn't do anything to stop it, paralysed by hurt and fear. She was crying and afraid—this wasn't like her. What was going on?

She rocked and leaned her head against her knees, praying she wasn't losing her mind. A sob escaped. She couldn't control anything, not even the loudness of her cries when two men were possibly still outside ready to burst back in.

"Baby, what's the matter?"

She heard Travis talking but he sounded so far away.

Shaking her head against the pain, she cried out to him.

"I…don't…know… So…scared…" She couldn't finish.

He sniffed the air around her, and she cowered away from him—it was like an infection was spreading through her body.

"You don't smell the same. There's something different about you," he said.

Suddenly she didn't like him being close. She tried to shuffle away from him then rocked back and forth.

"Daddy?" she called. He would take the bad and the hurt away. He would keep her safe, always.

"He's given you some sort of drug to make you feel crazy."

Sarah didn't know what he was talking about and she didn't care.

"Forgive me, baby," he whispered.

Forgive him? What for? What had he done?"

He moved her hair out of the way, trapped her arms at her side and kissed her neck. Seconds later, hot burning pain unlike anything else consumed her. Travis had bitten her neck and was sucking out her blood. He wasn't a vampire, wasn't a wolf right now, so what the hell was he doing? Sarah tried to keep her screams contained but it did no good. Her neck was being savaged by a man-beast and she couldn't stop him.

Before she knew what was happening, a scream released from her throat at the same time that the haze around her heart and eyes lifted. She could breathe and see clearly, the fear of moments ago banished.

She dropped to the truck bed when Travis let her go and he fell behind her, panting. She turned to him, her hand going to the bloody bite. She didn't care about the pain. Her concern was for Travis. He lay sweating and shaking.

"Travis? What's going on? What the fuck was that all about?"

"Ah, I see you've finally got him," Clark said loudly. "Perfect result, Rodney. I never thought your plan would work, but there you go."

Sarah turned, watching Clark and Rodney enter the barn. They looked smug and satisfied. She ignored them and touched Travis. He cowered from her touch.

"It's me, Travis. What's the matter?"

He stared past her shoulder, seemingly unhearing.

Heat spread from the wound at her neck and she winced. What the *fuck* was going on?

"What did you do to him?" She got to her feet to confront the two men who now looked at Travis with malicious intent in their eyes. Her hands shook from the loss of blood and her concern for Travis was distracting her.

"We did nothing, but it seems a little dose of experimental drugs did the trick with you." Clark smirked as both men walked closer. Both coming on either side.

"You're fucking sick!" Now she was pissed off, especially when Clark nodded, his gaze on Travis.

"He's too strong as a wolf and way too strong to contain as a man. Rodney figured, after watching the way you two are together, he'd come looking for you, so he left a trail of your scent, used some of your panties. Had him travelling like the dog he is."

Sarah knew she would burn every single item of clothing when she got home in case that creepy fucker had touched it all.

Disgusting bastards.

She knelt beside Travis and shook him.

"You need to turn, change to a wolf and you'll be fine." She sounded crazy saying that, but she'd think about this shifting shit later. She knew now he'd changed into a wolf to help mend the bullet wound in his foot. Whatever they'd given her, what he'd sucked out of her, could be dispersed the moment he changed, couldn't it?

And I thought he didn't care…

"No can do, honey." Clark pulled her by the arm away from Travis.

She snarled, yanked her arm back, spun round and slapped Clark across the face. "Don't call me honey. And don't you touch me, you fucking coward," she said, pummelling at him and striking any part of him she could.

Clark pushed her, and before Sarah could get her footing he slapped her face. The pain was quick and sharp and sent her sprawling from the truck bed onto the floor.

"I'm a coward?"

He walked to her and hauled her up by her hair. She could see Travis watching the scene and it broke her heart. He looked like he wanted to get up and do something to stop him but was too drugged up—and it was all her fault.

"Look at the man you were fucking earlier," Clark said. "Look at him, Sarah."

She cried out when he fisted her hair and his other hand grabbed her face and forced her to look at Travis.

"Let…her…go…" Travis managed, but it was obvious the struggle for him was tremendous.

"I like our Sarah, buddy. I'll keep her around for a little longer." Clark dragged her hair back and moved his hand holding her face to her breast.

He squeezed the mound, bringing tears to her eyes.

She screamed in anger again and spat at him, trying to get away. He pushed her to the floor before lifting her off the ground and handing her to Rodney.

"Keep that bitch secure." He stared right into her face. "Don't want you to have the same fate as Macy Jo, do we?"

Sarah jolted. "What about Macy? What the fuck have you done to her?" she yelled, fighting and cursing.

Rodney may have been a few cents short of a dollar, but he certainly made up for it in strength. She couldn't move—she tried to lash out and kick him but failed.

"Let's just say Macy has been taken for the greater good," Clark drawled. "Besides, you look at me like I'm the devil. Look at your man and see who killed Macy. Whose blood is on his hands?"

Sarah looked at Travis and knew he'd never do such a thing. He was too caring and he couldn't lash out at a woman. And as for the blood—there hadn't been any on him before he'd bitten her neck.

"You'll never get away with this," she snarled. "Stephen will know the truth and he'll find you. I'll tell him myself." Her heart was breaking. John—how would he cope knowing his wife was dead and gone?

How could anyone kill that sweet, loving woman? And she'd been pregnant!

"You think Stephen will stop me?" Clark roared with laughter. "My God, are you that stupid? Do you really think that's the only special medicine I've got? I've got stuff that'll keep you docile for a good few days, honey."

She gritted her teeth at his use of that name again. If she could get free, so help her God, she'd tear his eyes out.

Clark moved to Travis, taunting the other man with foul words. Rodney squeezed her a little tighter, showing her his strength, and she gasped at the sight of another man in the doorway.

"Clark, what am I doing here?" Stephen walked into the barn.

Sarah prayed he'd do the right thing.

"Stephen, right on time as always. I've got Travis here, the person who killed that hiker and Macy Jo and now he's going to kill you." Clark pulled out a gun and shot Stephen in the chest.

Sarah screamed, slammed her foot on Rodney's, and he let her go, cursing. She ran to Stephen and put her hand over the bullet wound. Blood was escaping through his mouth and he was gasping.

"Oh, God, what did you do?" she yelled at Clark.

He was kneeling next to Travis, forcing him to take the gun. This was too much.

"I'm sorry," Stephen gasped out before he took one final breath.

Sarah pulled away her blood-covered hands.

Stephen's blood. John, if he found out about Clark, would rip the man apart, but it looked like Clark would get away with this if she wasn't around to give evidence.

She didn't think. She looked at Stephen's lifeless body and saw his gun. She reached over and pretended to fix the sheriff's shirt and sobbed to muffle her movements.

She stood and turned the gun on Clark.

Sarah had no chance of leaving this barn alive unless she did this. She wouldn't be a slave to Clark and his disgusting cronies. The town deserved better than this piece of shit. It would end here, in this barn.

She might die anyway, but she'd take Clark with her.

Chapter Thirteen

What the hell was Sarah doing? Travis watched from his prone position, willing himself to get the hell up off the floor and step between her and Clark. His body felt like it had liquefied, though, and he was frustrated as fuck about it. His brain was functioning just fine, and if he could just get enough strength to call out, distract Clark…

But he couldn't waste time trying—and what if he distracted Sarah instead? He didn't need her worrying about him, not now—he needed to gather all the energy he could in order to shift. Pick the right moment to do it, too. He'd tried it several times while watching the woman he loved being manhandled by that jerk, and each time he'd failed to reach that place in his mind that enabled him to transform. His attention being on her instead was a killer, throwing his concentration off. If he could just shift, he'd be renewed, the drugs leeched out of his system from the changeover, his strength returned.

Sarah stood resolute facing Clark, gun pointing at him, and, God, he was proud of her—her hand didn't even shake, despite Stephen being dead on the ground. He cursed himself for being so out of it, no good to her when it mattered the most—no good to the sheriff. He should have realised Clark hadn't wandered off with Rodney and left the barn door open, should have known they were lulling him into a false sense of security, to draw him out of hiding so they could catch him. Then Stephen coming in like that… He'd looked spaced out, out of his tree on drugs—and then to be killed?

Fucking hell.

How the fuck was Travis going to deal with watching Sarah kill a man while he lay idly by? It was his job to protect her, God damn it, not the other way around. Being incapacitated burned him so badly he felt sick.

"I'll fucking kill you if you take one step closer," Sarah said. "You've fucked with me one time too many. How the hell dare you, getting your pathetic friend to bring me here, feeling me up while he was at it?"

"Felt you up, did he?" Clark grimaced and looked at Rodney. "Did you touch her, fuckface?"

Rodney blushed, clasping his hands behind his back like a recalcitrant schoolboy, and stared at the dusty floor.

"You did, didn't you?" Clark spat a glob of phlegm on the floor. "I expressly told you not to do anything like that. She's mine, God damn it. Bad enough freaky wolf boy there's been in her hole before me." He ground his teeth then sighed. "Still, sloppy seconds is better than none at all. I'll deal with you later, Rodney. You've gone and pissed me the hell off, and you know what that means, right?"

"Yes, boss. Sorry, boss."

Clark mimicked him then returned his attention to Sarah. "So, as you were saying?"

"Fuck you," she said.

"Oh, that'll come later, honey, don't you worry yourself about that."

"It won't. You'll never touch me again."

"Oh yeah?" Clark smirked.

If she doesn't kill you first, I'll wipe that smirk right off your butt-ugly face.

"Yeah, so back the hell off!" Sarah warned.

"You won't shoot me. Not when Rodney here can overpower you. He may look as thick as pig's shit, but, as you've seen already, he's mighty strong when he has to be."

Shit!

Rodney was looking to Clark for guidance, but his 'boss' wasn't giving him any hints, his sights set firmly on Sarah.

Clark jerked his head sideways, gaze still on Sarah, a smug smile on his face. "Go and sort that dead-as-a-doornail asshole out, dickwad. Drag him outside. Never should have been made sheriff, that one. Deputy had his head stuck up his ass when he brought Stephen on board. I told him to take me on instead, but, no, he reckoned I had a tight enough grip on the town already. And I do." He chuckled, shaking his head.

Rodney appeared downcast, as though he'd been itching for the chance to grab Sarah and press himself against her. Damn pervert freak. If they got through this, Travis imagined Sarah would take a while to forget the feel of those men touching her. Earlier, when she'd mentioned being groped by them, he'd had to rein in his anger, had to stop himself from rushing out of the barn and attacking them.

So why didn't you? Why the fuck didn't you?

Because he'd wanted to stay with Sarah, to give her comfort, keep her safe.

And now look what's happened. If you'd have just gone for them, torn out their damn throats like you've threatened, she wouldn't be standing there now with a gun in her hand and some asshole goading her to shoot him.

"Well? What the fuck are you still doing here?" Clark shouted. "Go sort out the damn sheriff, you hear me?"

Rodney pursed his lips, gave Sarah a long, lingering look, shrugged and hunkered down. He tucked his hands into Stephen's armpits and dragged the corpse outside. A trail of blood marred the floor now, and Stephen's heels had left two slim ravines through the dust. Travis blew out a sigh of relief that the threat to Sarah had lessened, but what about Stephen? Where the hell would Rodney take him?

"So, *honey.*" Clark took a step backwards, his boot sole making the grit beneath it crackle. He looked down and toed the ground, acting as though bored, that taking his gaze off her really didn't faze him. And maybe it didn't. Maybe he was so sure of himself that he didn't fear her in the slightest. "Take a shot, sweetness. See where you hit. See if all your bluster about having a gun in every room is worth the effort it took for you to tell everyone about them."

Sarah stared at him, eyes narrowed, her cheeks flushing the claret of an angry woman. He knew all about her temper, how Clark's words would have pissed her off. He imagined her mind ticking over, her thinking of where she could shoot Clark so he didn't die—so he'd still have to live and suffer in jail with men who wouldn't hesitate to beat the crap out of him on a daily basis for what he'd done. Killing a hiker was bad enough, but taking a mother away from two small kids? Clark wouldn't stand a chance.

Travis smiled wryly and a burst of pride surged through him. She may be as stubborn as a damn mule, but it had got her somewhere in life—a respected ranch owner who took no shit from her workers. He'd wager she was asking herself if she could do it—if she could kill a man even though he was bad to the bone.

"You go ahead and take your time, honey. I got all day." Clark dug a hand in his pocket and brought out a box of matches. "I'll just go and sit right over here, and, when you're ready, you go on and pull that trigger."

He's mocking her, the son of a bitch!

Clark sat on an empty wooden barrel and took a match out of the box, inserting it between his disgusting teeth. Travis expected him to strike another match and toss it towards the hay bales in the far corner, but the man put the box back in his pocket and crossed his arms over his chest. He stretched his legs out and hooked one ankle over the other, looking as if he was just passing away some spare time.

He's got some fucking balls. But she'll do it if she's pushed. She'll shoot you, motherfucker. Go on, push her. See what she's made of.

But Clark didn't speak, just picked at his teeth with the match, studying the end to see if his rooting around had produced anything. Sarah remained in place, finger curled around the half-cocked trigger, gaze staunch, unwavering. Her mouth twitched as if she was going to say something but nothing came out. She'd thought better of it, then.

This is your chance. Ignore them. Close your mind off. Get to where you need to be.

Travis closed his eyes. The barn was silent except for their breathing and the *flick-flick-flick* of that match against the bastard's teeth. He focused so hard a pain jabbed the back of his head, but he pushed on, reaching out to that special place in the shadowy recesses of his mind. He grasped its edges and held on, pulling on it, dragging it towards him until its warm thickness enveloped him. It cosseted, caressed, and spread through him like a shot of fast-downed rye, freeing his limbs from the lethargy that had claimed them. And then his bones minimised, forming those that would knit together with muscle and sinew to create the skeleton and innards of his wolf. A shot of adrenaline ricocheted through his blood, speeding to nerve endings and sparking the energy he'd longed to possess. Hair sprouted, popping through his skin, and his fingernails strained as they changed into claws.

He opened his eyes, thanking the good Lord above that he looked down on his sprawled wolf form. Quietly, filled with vigour and an excess of power, he got up on all fours, adopting the stance to pounce.

Sarah remained staring at Clark.

Clark remained chewing his matchstick from his perch on the barrel.

Travis made a quick-fire decision. He crept around the front of his truck and down the other side so he was closer to Clark. Hoping his paw pads didn't encounter anything on the floor that would make a noise, he slunk forward one slow, agonising step at a time, and stopped just before the end of his truck bed.

Clark sighed and glanced up at the ceiling, clearly playing at being bored.

Travis sniffed, caught Sarah's attention. She gave him a wide-eyed stare but kept the gun in place.

Clark lifted both hands to rub his eyes with square-ended fingertips.

Big mistake, fucker.

Travis lunged, leaping through the air at incredible speed and slamming into Clark. Clark toppled sideways, the thud of him hitting the floor a pleasure to Travis' ears. Travis jumped on top of him, pinning him in place on his back. There was no question of what he was going to do—no question at all.

Praying Sarah had the instinct to look away, Travis lowered his head in a swift-as-fuck movement and filled his mouth with Clark's neck. The bastard writhed, struck Travis' back with hard fists and gurgled in protest. Travis bit—hard—and, without even a glimmer of remorse, gave a flick of his head. The click of Clark's windpipe snapping was almost lost in the louder noise of flesh being ripped free. Travis growled and snarled, hating the taste of the man's blood on his tongue but continuing just the same.

No one threatened his woman. No one.

Travis flung Clark's flesh to the side and stepped off him, padding to the barn doorway without a backward glance as Sarah gulped in huge breaths behind him. He'd comfort her as soon as this was really over. He couldn't give in and go to her now. Although Rodney was a dumb son of a bitch, he was still dangerous. Travis looked back at Sarah, who glared at Clark's jerking body then slowly faced Travis.

"Jesus Christ," she whispered. "You ripped his fucking throat out!"

Travis nodded once, turning away to peek around the door frame. Rodney stood halfway between the barn and the cottage, appearing to try to lift Stephen up to the lip of Travis' well. The sheriff's body was having none of it, seeming to push at him, arm swinging by itself, swatting the dimwit on his chest. Rodney struggled on in his usual docile manner, but then abruptly his demeanour changed. He went from buddy-buddy to all-out mean, launching an uppercut to the sheriff's jaw. Stephen's head snapped back, and Rodney let him go. The sheriff went down like a sack of shit, his ass meeting the ground with a bone-jarring smack.

"I gotta sort you," Rodney said. "Now, I tried being nice, and look how ungrateful you were." He swung back his leg, ready to kick.

Travis had seen enough. He darted forward, reaching the pair within a second. Barrelling his head into Rodney's back, he sent the man flying. Rodney yelled out a strangled "What the fuck?" before landing face-first in the dirt. Travis held him down, two legs either side of him, and looked to his right at Stephen.

The sheriff was a pitiful sight. Travis shifted quickly, reached for the handcuffs dangling from the man's belt and secured Rodney's wrists in metal. Travis glanced around, spying the bucket chain hanging from the underside of the well roof, nodded to himself and yanked Rodney to his feet. He forced Rodney to the well and manacled him to the chain.

Back inside the barn, he checked to see if Clark had stopped moving before he returned to his corner. The man was dead, no doubt about that, and, without any more hesitation, Travis stared out of the barn doorway and whispered to Sarah, "Quickly, while I keep watch in case someone heard the gunshot. In my truck there's water. A bottle of it in the glove box. The truck's open. Hurry!"

She didn't stop to question—*halle-goddamn-lujah!*—and rushed over to the truck, swinging the door wide and producing the water he needed. He took it, dousing his face, cleaning away the blood that would give him away, then tossed the bottle back through the open truck doorway.

As he lowered to the floor he said, "Close the truck door, honey, then go and get the deputy. Explain what happened. Tell him I'm still groggy."

She didn't argue, running out of the barn. He watched her come abreast of Rodney and speak, then look him up and down. She kicked him full force in his bollocks, spitting on him as he jerked around in pain.

She disappeared for a while, returning with the deputy in tow.

"You okay there, buddy?" the deputy asked.

"Yeah, yeah, but he isn't." Travis nodded across the way.

The deputy followed his movement. "Jesus H. Christ. That damn wolf sure had a bite on him."

"Aww, God," Rodney wailed from outside. "Aww, boss!"

"Oh, give me a damn break," Sarah shouted back, strutting towards Travis. "He's where he ought to be—in Hell—and you'll be joining him if you don't shut the fuck up!"

"Where did the wolf go?" the deputy asked, eyes going left to right.

"Hell if I know," Sarah said, hunkering down beside Travis. "All I care about is getting my man some clothes, taking him home where he can recuperate." She cocked her head and tucked strands of his hair behind his ear. "You okay, wolf boy?" she whispered.

Travis almost laughed but caught himself just in time. Feigning tiredness, he made a song and dance of struggling to stand. "Just let me get some clothes so I can cover my nuts up."

Sarah put a hand around his waist and he leaned on her for support.

"So why are you naked, anyway?" the deputy asked.

"I was stripped by Rodney last night. Sarah told you that, right?" Travis said.

Rodney wailed again.

"Like I said," Sarah muttered, "shut the fuck up, Rodney."

"Let me…" Travis breathed heavily as though tired. "Let me talk to him."

The deputy stared at Travis. "Two minutes." He stood over Clark and tugged his radio off his belt.

Travis walked outside with Sarah, leaned close to Rodney, mouth by his ear. "If you so much as breathe a word about me being out at Gordon's Creek last night—or even out at all—you remember your boss, yeah?"

Travis drew back, his nose inches from the other man's. Rodney nodded.

"I'll fucking rip *your* throat out like that as well."

* * * *

"So, let me get this right," the deputy said, pacing up and down Sarah's living room. "Clark killed Macy Jo and Stephen, Rodney kidnapped Sarah, and he also drugged you? Smacked you on the back of the head then stripped you naked?"

"That's about the gist of it, yeah," Travis said, clothed in his well-worn jeans and soft plaid shirt.

"What the hell for?" the deputy asked, frowning deeply.

"No damn clue. Who knows what goes on in the mind of someone like him?" Travis sniffed and rubbed his jaw.

"And some wolf killed Clark?" The deputy paused in his pacing and stared at Travis and Sarah.

"Yes, I saw it," Sarah said. "It frightened me to death." She bit her bottom lip.

"I'll just bet it did," the deputy said. "Well, it's all a bunch of mess and no mistake, but I'll file the reports and we'll see what the magistrate says. I can't see Rodney getting jailed. Diminished responsibility is on the cards, you'll see. The man's a jabbering wreck, saying you're the wolf and you threatened to rip *his* throat out."

"Oh, give me strength!" Travis slapped his thigh.

"I know. Crazy is as crazy does, right? The guy's clearly nuts."

"Clearly," Sarah said, pressing a fingertip to her lips.

"Well, I'll thank you for the tea and be on my way. A lot of paperwork is in my future. It goes without saying that you don't leave the county until a decision's been made as to whether Rodney stands trial—not that I think you've got anything to do with this in a bad way, of course."

"Of course." Travis stood and shook the deputy's hand. "I'm not going anywhere." He glanced down at Sarah and caught her soft smile. "I've got my woman here to look after and the men to reinstate. We've got a ranch to run."

"Ah, so you'll be sticking around for a while yet, then?" The deputy nodded to himself as if pleased with what he'd heard.

"Yep. We need to get stuck in and get this place fixed up, and Sarah here's going to be taking a back seat."

"She is?"

"I am?"

Travis chuckled. "Damn right you are." He smiled at her warmly, a glut of love spreading like unruly ivy through his body. "It's about time you let a man take some weight off your shoulders."

The deputy cleared his throat. "I'll, uh, be off then. See myself out."

Travis waited until he heard the front door close softly then sat beside Sarah.

"Before you protest, honey, just hear me out."

"Ooh, I could slap you for what you just said. A man taking some of the weight off my shoulders, my ass. Just who do you think you are, Travis Williams?"

"The man who's going to carry that weight."

She widened her eyes—eyes that looked a little watery. "Shit, Travis, I…"

"You're not getting rid of me, Sarah French. No damn way." He pulled her to him, gliding his fingers through her soft hair and kissing the top of her head. "So, my first order—one you're going to obey—"

"Obey!" She jerked back. "Why, you cheeky son of a bitch!"

He laughed and kissed her nose. "As I was saying… My first order is that we go and meet with John, see if he needs any help with Macy Jo's funeral. After that, we're going to call on every man you employed and ask them to come back—"

"I can do that. I want to do that." She squeezed his hand tightly.

"All right, that's fine. You can do that if it makes you happy. And then…"

He paused.

"And then?"

"I'm going to bring you home and take you to bed…for a very long time."

Chapter Fourteen

John was an emotional wreck, chanting to himself.

"When she didn't come home I knew something was wrong, Sarah. Even though she stayed out sometimes, I felt it, right here." He thumped his chest.

Sarah's heart broke a little bit more to see such a tough man brought to his knees by the terrifying news of the death of his woman and unborn child.

"If you need anything at all, just call me." Sarah put a reassuring hand over his and squeezed, trying with all her might to give him strength.

He nodded but refused to look at her.

Travis stood behind her, offering her his strength with a hand on her shoulder. They'd figured the news would best be broken by her rather than a total stranger—the deputy had agreed this was the right way to do it.

Sarah wasn't so sure.

"It was Clark, wasn't it?" John asked, murder in his eyes.

"How do you know?" she whispered.

"Macy phoned me last night, told me Clark was causing trouble. I fucking hated that prick, even though it looked like we were buddies. It was better that way, made him easier to deal with. If I ever get my hands on him he'll be fuckin' dead."

Sarah knew he *would* kill him as well. John had been completely devoted to Macy.

"I'm sorry, buddy. A wolf already took care of his useless, lying ass," Travis said.

Sarah had never felt so much relief to have a scumbag dead. She shivered just remembering Clark's hands on her and the intention in his eyes. She was so pleased he'd never got the chance to carry out his threats.

"It was too easy. He deserved more pain." John sighed, his whole body shuddering.

Sarah couldn't have agreed more, but Clark was dead and gone and he'd left a trail of horror in his wake. Macy Jo would always be missed—her presence had been felt by everyone in town.

Half an hour later, Sarah and Travis left with the promise that John would keep in touch. Sarah may not have liked him all that much, but Macy Jo would have wanted her to make sure he was taken care of.

In the car, Sarah and Travis travelled in silence. Already there was a difference in the people. Sombre expressions and nervousness had spread like wildfire. News and gossip sure did move quickly.

Sarah decided to fill the silence. She couldn't cope with all the quiet. She liked to hear noise when she was upset—it took her mind off things. "They all know something."

"How can you be certain?"

"This is a small town and news travels fast. If they don't know exactly what's going on, it won't take them long to figure it out. Macy Jo and Stephen are both dead. They were prominent people. Ones who will be missed." She stopped, her voice wobbling. It would be hard for the next few months to not think of Macy. Stephen hadn't always been the best sheriff but he'd tried. She wondered what John would do with the bar.

"I'm sorry about your friends, but please don't cry." Travis took one hand from the steering wheel and held hers.

But nothing could stop the hurt inside.

In the moment, she hadn't had time to assess what had taken place, but now that she could think and process, the tears began. She covered her face with her hands and allowed emotion to swamp her. She heard Travis pull his truck to the side of the road. Rodney had stolen hers when he'd kidnapped her.

"Let me hold you," he murmured, placing his arms around her shoulders and bringing her closer to him.

Sarah released her sobs, her sadness at losing two people she'd known—one of whom she'd loved.

"I don't know why I'm crying now, why I didn't cry at the time," she said, tears welling further.

He shushed her, rocked her, stroking her hair. She cried and got comfort from his arms.

"You've had a lot of shocks today, baby, just let it go. I've got you and I'll never let anyone hurt you."

His words soothed and calmed, allowing her time to simply mourn. She knew she wouldn't get over it straight away, but, like everything else in life, you couldn't take a time-out from living. Bills still needed to be paid.

At least in his arms, for this short period of time, she could just breathe.

"I love you, Travis," she confessed.

She didn't expect a matching answer from him, but she'd wanted to tell him for a while now. She couldn't recall how far back or even when she'd started to love him. All she knew was, when she thought of losing him, she never wanted him to go.

Travis tensed his arms around her, and Sarah jerked back to look at him.

"I didn't say it for you to say anything," she said. "I mean, it doesn't matter if you don't love me. I just wanted you to know I love you." She pulled away and stared out of the window. "I'm ready to go and see the men."

Drive, please just drive.

Times like this, she wished she could see inside his head. To have a small speck of understanding as to what he was thinking. He brushed her hair out of the way, and Sarah made sure she didn't respond even if all she wanted to do was lean her cheek against his hand and kiss him.

"Sarah, honey, look at me."

The large truck suddenly felt small and cold. She shook her head, heard a rustle of movement, then Travis took her face in his hands and turned her, a little by force, to face him. He rubbed each remaining tear from her cheeks and took her lips in a slow, sensual kiss. Sarah was determined not to respond.

Why am I doing this? Why can't I just stop being so stubborn?

He tilted her head, exposing her neck. She still refused to respond, but the reaction of her body was already creating a path of fire. Butterflies fluttered in her belly. Her nipples budded, the material of her shirt abrading them. Her clit pulsed, juices flooding from her cunt, swamping her panties with cream. She wanted Travis and no matter what she thought about she couldn't stop him from swamping her with need. Within seconds, she couldn't fight anymore and gave up to the power of his lips. He moved his hand to the back of her head and sank his fingers in the long strands. She moaned with the force of lust his touch produced, bliss going straight to her core.

She closed her legs, the friction rubbing her nub to delightful heights. Her moan and gasp opened her mouth, and Travis took advantage of her vulnerability. He thrust his tongue between her lips and into her mouth. She tasted him on her tongue and moaned again, the meeting of lips becoming brutal with their onslaught of passion.

She needed him now. She couldn't wait any longer. Sarah moved her hand over his groin and massaged his stiff shaft. Already he was hot and ready, and heat spread to her palm through the restrictive clothing.

"Get a room!" Someone banged on the side of the truck, making them jerk apart, panting for breath and smiling.

"We need to talk to your men first, honey. I promised to make love to you, and I damn well don't break promises."

Travis started the truck, and Sarah was relieved to see his hands shaking—he was as affected by them being together as she was. She licked her lips and moaned again, his flavour erupting on her tongue and driving her crazy with longing.

"When I get you home, I'm going to fuck you in every room of the house," Travis said.

Sarah placed her hand between her legs and squeezed tightly, the flush building and spreading inside her. "Are you really?"

"Are you going to stop me?"

Travis didn't take his gaze away from the road, and Sarah knew, whatever he wanted, she would do it.

"I'd never dream of stopping you." She leaned her head back and removed her hands. There would be time for that later. She didn't want to be turned on when she faced a diner full of men.

"Where do you think your men will be?"

"At the diner, nursing some pie and coffee, waiting for me to come and give them their jobs back."

Just like her father had done before her. Sarah remembered him doing the same crazy stunt several years back. She couldn't recall what had happened for her father to lose his cool but he had, firing all of his men at the same time. On the same day, he'd arranged to meet the men at the diner. Sarah had driven him out to apologise and get his workers back, paying for lunch as well.

A few minutes later, Travis pulled up outside the diner. Sarah peered through the windows. All of her workers were there, and, yes, they nursed coffee and pie. Absurdly, she wondered if it was cherry or apple.

She took a deep breath and turned to Travis. "Maybe I should do this alone?"

He was already shaking his head and leaving the truck. "I don't think so, honey. We're in this together, remember?" He came round and helped her out, stayed close and guided her down, but instead of getting out of her way he pushed her against the truck so anyone watching could see.

"What are you doing?" she asked.

She glanced around. People were staring at them, and she didn't like to have all that attention.

"Showing those men whose woman you are and that I'm back. They'll respect me for bringing you here and you for bringing me along. You got rid of them because you thought I'd left you, and, baby..." He cupped her cheek and forced her to look him in the eye.

Sarah saw determination and the message he was trying to get across.

He was going through this with her whether she liked it or not.

"I think I've given you a little too much control," she teased, moving her hands around his neck and rubbing her breasts against his chest.

His eyes dilated, and he dropped his gaze to her heaving mounds.

"Huh, and here I thought you were over me."

He cupped her ass, rubbing her cunt on his hard-on. "I'm never going to get tired of you, honey. Now let's go and get you your workers back."

He swatted her ass. She yelped and glared at him.

He just smacked me on the ass!

She kind of liked it, and was that so bad?

He chuckled and followed her into the diner. A few other people ate lunch, but her workers were spread over four tables close together. The older ones looked at their watches and glanced her way.

"You're a little late, sweetheart," the oldest man said.

Sarah couldn't stop the smile. "Sorry, but I got held up."

"You here to stay, Travis?" he asked.

The men looked at Travis behind her, and Sarah saw the respect they already had for him. She wondered what would have happened if he'd come back and not stayed with her. She would never wonder about that again—Travis Williams was all hers and he'd be hers for a good long while.

"Yes, sir, I am." Travis took her hand.

The men grunted and each looked at the others.

"I'm sorry what I did, guys, I really am," she said.

"Miss French," the old man said. "I worked for your father and I watched you grow from a fine young girl into a beautiful, fair and sometimes temperamental woman. Now, these younger men thought they'd lost their job over that Clark boy. I want you to assure them that, like your father before you, you'll be prone to your tempers, but come the afternoon or the next day we'll all be back in a job."

What a way to feel like a bitch.

"I swear I won't do anything like that again, I—"

"Gentlemen, this morning was my fault," Travis said. "I wasn't there—no doubt you'll hear all about it soon if you haven't already. My lady thought I'd left her, and she took her anger out on you. Anyway, I can promise you, from here on out, Sarah will be directing all of her little moods my way—and only my way. Now, before we move on with getting you guys back to work, I have something else I want to do first."

Travis went down on one knee before the whole diner. With her heart thumping, the diners silent, Travis took her hand.

She held her breath as he gazed up at her. He was so handsome and sexy and this couldn't be happening. She'd pinch herself later.

"Miss Sarah French, I know we haven't known each other for a long time, but I can swear on everything I am that I love you and I want to spend the rest of my life being with you. I want you to have my babies and be with me when I grow old. I can't guarantee life will always be easy, but I *can* guarantee you'll own my heart. Please, would you do me the honour of becoming my wife? My one and only?"

Music—all she could hear was wonderful music.

"Is she alive stood there?" the old man yelled.

"Maybe she didn't hear you," another said.

"I'll marry ya, Travis, if she doesn't."

She heard all their words but only had eyes for Travis. She loved everything about him, the man and the wolf. She'd willingly take everything he had to offer her and more.

"What's it to be, honey?"

"Yes," she whispered.

His proposal and the day seemed so surreal. She took her hand out of his and pinched herself.

"Ouch."

Travis got to his feet and kissed her hand. "This is the real deal. No joking. I want you forever."

"Yes, yes, yes," she said, flinging herself at him. She was so happy, and the tears this time were from joy. She couldn't believe how much she'd gained in such a short time.

The old man got up and offered them his congratulations. "She'll be a handful."

They all warned him, but Sarah knew in her heart that Travis was up to the challenge.

She smiled at him, heart full to bursting, her knees a little weak and new butterflies taking flight inside her. Travis kissed her neck and whispered beautiful words of love in her ear.

"Let's celebrate with more coffee and more pie," one of the workers shouted to the room.

Sarah laughed. "Which flavour?"

"Apple."

Yum, her favourite.

* * * *

They stayed and ate pie, Sarah holding Travis' hand the whole time. Women came into the diner as soon as they heard the news and congratulated her. Everyone wanted to be a bridesmaid, but by the end of an hour Sarah just wanted to go home, be fucked, then travel to Vegas to get married in one of those quick and cheap bridal shops.

Travis drove home, the sexual tension mounting with every passing second. Her pussy was driving her crazy, and the need to have Travis fucking her was so intense she felt she would weep if he didn't drive faster.

He parked the truck and she looked at the house. It would need to be cleaned because of Rodney touching her things.

"How's your hand?" he asked suddenly.

Sarah glanced down, shocked to feel that it didn't hurt much under the fresh bandage she'd wrapped around her palm earlier. She removed the gauze.

"Wow. It's almost healed."

"There are some things you'll need to know about me, honey, things I'll tell you as time goes by, but your healing…that's from my saliva. When I bit you, it entered the wound, gave you faster healing properties. It's handy being a wolf sometimes."

He grinned but seemed a little distant, gazing into space. Sarah glanced at the house again, wondering why his mood had gone down.

"What's the matter?" she asked.

He'd promised to fuck her in every room of that house and she wanted that. After the past two days, all she wanted to do was end this one by being in bed with him.

"I should have been there for you," he said quietly. "Rodney and Clark should have never gotten the chance..."

Sarah understood his concern. "I'm fine, really, Travis." She placed a hand on his cheek and implored him with her eyes to believe her.

"Do you really want to marry a wolf?"

His vulnerability was showing through.

Sarah leaned over and took his face in her palms. "I love you, Travis, the man not the wolf. Okay, if you start howling at the moon and going seriously furry all the damn time I'll have a problem, but you, like this, I love you. I don't care about the wolf thing." She kissed him then pulled back and smiled. "You'd better warn me, though, if I'm expected to give birth to a pack of little wolves. *Then* I'll have an issue."

Travis laughed and exited the truck.

Please let him take me out of the truck and into the house and fuck me. I'm dying here.

Travis opened her door and took her in his arms. He was so strong, wasn't straining in carrying her over the threshold. She giggled as he made his way straight upstairs.

"I thought you said every room?" she teased.

He didn't reply, but instead of taking her to the bedroom, he moved to the bathroom.

"Come on, Travis, I'm desperate here," she complained.

He sat her on the toilet seat and went about running a bath. He didn't talk to her but continued to work around her. Lavender bath soap was added to the tub, creating bubbles in the water. He tested the temperature then came to her. He pulled her to her feet and kissed her.

"I'm going to clean you and love you, honey."

How could she protest when all of his attention was on her?

He lifted her shirt out of the way, not taking any notice of her plain bra, then dropped to his knees. He removed her boots and socks, then unzipped her jeans, and she held his shoulders to lift one leg then the other as he pulled them down and off, followed by her plain panties. Never before in her life had a man treated her this way.

"Please hurry, Travis," she begged.

"Not yet." Travis came back up and removed her bra, stroking his thumb over a pointed nipple. His gaze remained on her.

Her body was on fire and he wanted to bathe it. So not fair.

He picked her up in his powerful arms and lowered her into the tub. She expected the water to be steaming but it was lovely and warm and the bubbles surrounded her. Closing her eyes and leaning back, she moaned, her muscles suddenly protesting. Maybe a bath was a good idea after all. With his hands on her shoulders, he moved her forward, and she opened her eyes to watch Travis' naked ass as he joined her. He got in behind her, his hard cock pressing against the base of her back.

She tried to turn but he held her steady and, taking a cloth, slowly washed her.

"I want to take care of you," he whispered.

She leant back and let him touch. He hummed in her ear and washed her hair, every touch made with the intention to soothe. He ran his fingers through her hair, working the knots out. Her muscles were already Jell-O, and she loved every second.

Finally, after what seemed a lifetime, he cupped her breasts. She arched back and groaned.

"Your breasts are the thing of dreams." He stroked and fondled the mounds of flesh.

"What're you doing to me?" she whispered.

He trailed his hands down her ribcage and back up, his intention to tease every last bit of tension out of her, she was sure of it.

"Please, Travis."

"I'm loving you, Sarah. Relax and let me show you what true loving is all about."

Sarah watched him work over her body. She arched, not caring about the water, whether it sloshed onto the floor. All she wanted was Travis and his touch.

"You have such a pretty pussy. I've fantasised about sucking your cream out of your cunt."

Sarah gasped at his word choice—so naughty, so rude, but, fuck, she liked it.

"I want you always," she said. "Please, Travis, show me everything. Teach me everything."

He stopped touching her, lifting his hands away, and Sarah looked up at him. His eyes shone brightly, the love clearly written in them.

"I love you, Sarah. And me not touching you? It's killing you, right?"

She loved hearing those three words, had waited a lifetime to hear them. "I love you too, and yes, you're killing me."

He stroked her cheek and grazed his thumb along her lips. "That's how it's always going to be, you wanting me like this. I'll make damn sure of it."

He pushed his thumb inside, and she touched him with her tongue.

"Do you trust me?" he asked.

"With my life."

There was no hesitation. She anticipated what he had in mind for the rest of their lives together. She loved him, and, no matter what, he had her love and trust.

Chapter Fifteen

Having washed and tended to Sarah in the bath with deliberate slowness, Travis dried her the same way, drawing the towel over every speck of her skin. She groaned, moaned and growled her frustration, so he slowed some more. He wanted her desperate, her cunt dripping for him, her nipples on those gorgeous tits of hers hard and wanting.

"Travis, I—"

"Hush, honey. Just let me do this. Just feel."

She stood beside the bath, legs slightly parted, arms loose by her sides, and he wanted more than anything to turn her around, bend her over that damn tub and sink his cock inside her heat, balls deep. This was as much a test for him as it was for her. He needed her to know that he would treat her right, arouse her for a long time before taking her the way his body screamed he should. Hard and fast, relentless thrusts that jerked her body—but she wasn't ready for that roughness, not yet. She was so new to this, and although she'd coped well when he'd taken her virginity and the times afterwards, he wasn't a fool. It would hurt her again this time, though not as much, and if she was as relaxed as she could get and sopping with her tangy cream, it would ease his way and soothe any pain.

God, he loved her, thanked God for her stubborn streak despite how much it had grated on him in the past. With all they'd been through, she was still strong, but he knew the demons would lurk in her mind, jump out at her when she least expected them—and he'd be there to soothe her when nightmares took their evil hold.

He knelt in front of her, brushing the towel over the dense hairs covering her mound, and fuck, his cock ached. His balls drew up, asshole puckering, and he counted to ten in an effort to take the edge off his lust as he dried her damp curls. Difficult, though, when her heady, womanly scent came towards him from between plump cunt lips that begged for him to taste them. To lave his tongue from the bottom of her slit to the top, twirling the tip around her throbbing clit until she snatched in a breath and whimpered.

Fuck.

He rose, unable to remain in control down there, and tossed the towel over the side of the empty tub. He took a step back to appraise her, noting how she blushed under his gaze. Not so outspoken now, was she? He felt a pinch of guilt for thinking like that, but his woman had a lot to learn—to be less impulsive at times, to think before she opened her mouth, to employ a bit of give and take. Yet…he shouldn't want to change her. He'd fallen in love with the woman she was and would continue to love her until his dying day.

She looked back at him, and he'd swear they were talking without words, gazes saying so much more than any sentence he could string together. A connection of souls. His old friends and pack he'd left behind when he'd come here would have ribbed him about that, but, shit, when a man was in love he didn't care what his buddies thought. No, all he cared about was the woman standing in front of him, keeping her safe. His.

He broke eye contact, taking another step back to see how she was handling what might appear as offhand perusal. He had a sense she wasn't completely comfortable with her body, and right now he wanted her to *become* more comfortable, to accept him eyeing her from head to toe and loving every goddamn dip and curve she owned.

"You're beautiful," he murmured.

"No, I'm not, I have large thighs and—"

"They're beautiful. All of you is beautiful."

He swept his gaze from her collarbone to the first hint at the rise of her breasts, lingering there so she could stare back at him in the same way, hoping she knew he wouldn't look up to catch her. She could learn from this experience, too, take in the male form, rake her gaze over his rigid cock and taut bollocks, and maybe, just maybe that would give her a little more confidence.

Her tits, Christ, they turned him on, all ripe swells and perky nipples. She jutted them out, a silent invitation for him to swoop his head and suck one hard-as-fuck bud into his mouth.

"You like what you see?" he asked softly, shifting his gaze lower to her navel then further down to the triangular thatch that had tempted him moments ago.

"Yes."

He didn't dare glance up at her face. "You just keep looking. It's all yours." He paused, seeing her legs tremble—from desire or cold he wasn't sure—then asked, "You like me looking at you like this? Like me staring at your cunt, at the way your hairs are wet because you want my cock inside you?"

"No... Yes... It's...embarrassing."

"You need to stop feeling embarrassed then, honey, because I plan on looking at you a lot. Think about how you feel when you look at me. Tell me how it feels."

"It's... Christ, Travis, I can't. I've never—"

"Then now's the time to start. Take a deep breath, close your eyes if you have to, and tell me how you feel."

Her intake of breath, full of judders and apprehension, brought a spike of remorse to his heart. Was he being too forceful, too soon? No, she had to learn to accept his appreciation—and he needed her boldness in the bedroom.

"I feel... It makes me want to touch you."

"What else?"

"I want to suck you. Lick you."

"And?"

"And I want you to do the same to me."

"How? What do you want?"

Her cunt lips spasmed. *God, I want to plunge my cock inside there and ride her until she screams.*

She sighed. "I...uh, I want you to lick me. There."

"Where?"

"*There!*"

"Say it. Say the word." His sac bunched then relaxed, balls heavy inside, aching with his need for release.

If she said what he wanted, he'd know his intuition had been right—she had to be drawn out of her shell, taught to explore, to find the courage to ask for what she needed. Oh, he'd learn what she needed given time, but he preferred a woman to know and not be afraid to ask.

"I can't say that!" Her voice sounded as though she stood on the border between excruciating awkwardness and wanting to run away and hide.

No way was she running. He wouldn't allow it. Although this lesson may be torture, she'd thank him for it later.

"Yes, you can. If you want me to do those things to you, then tell me what you want. Say the word. What do you want me to lick?"

"My… Oh, God. My… I want you to lick my…"

The sound of her hitching breaths filled the room. His pulse thudded in his ears. He clenched his hands, digging his nails into his palms, and willed himself to calm the hell down. He was torturing himself as well as her, prolonging the wait before that moment when he would touch her and everything would happen in a mad rush.

"Cunt," she whispered.

Oh, sweet Jesus, if he glanced up now he'd be undone. His cocked ached fiercely, blood swelling it further, and his slit stretched. He felt a drop of pre-cum ooze from it and dribble down the head, wishing she'd kneel and lick it away.

If he didn't watch himself he'd shoot his fucking load.

"You want me to lick your cunt?" he asked. "Lick right inside that juicy little slit of yours?"

"Oh, God, yes."

And, fuck, he wanted her to want his tongue there. Now.

"What else do you feel?" His voice came out raspy, his need soaking the words.

Her sweet cunt called to him, the scent of her arousal almost too strong to ignore. Her sex lips quivered again, and he reached out, sluicing one fingertip through her folds. She gasped—a sharp, painful-sounding inhalation—and bunched her hands into fists.

"Ah, you love that, right?" *I love it. I goddamn love it.*

"Yes," she whispered. "More."

"There. See?" He swirled his fingertip around her clit—once, twice. "That wasn't so bad, was it? Asking for more?"

"No."

"So, speak to me. Tell me *exactly* what you want." He applied a little more pressure, swirled again and again.

"I can't. It's too…rude."

"Nothing's rude around me, honey."

He circled again then brushed his thumb over her clit, pushing lightly until she hauled in another breath and staggered a bit. He waited for her to regain her composure, and as she did, she parted her legs some more.

"That's it, baby. You *do* know what you want."

"I want… Don't look at me when I say this."

"I promise I'll keep my eyes on your sexy, cream-filled cunt."

"Oh, God, the way you speak to me like that. It's… I like it."

"Good. And?"

She opened her legs wider, releasing a breathy *'Ah!'* "And when you…when you touch me like that I can't—oh!—breathe. I can't—ah!—think."

"And?" He rubbed faster, her clit swelling beneath his thumb.

"And I… When you…when you tapped my ass outside the…diner I…" She jerked her hips towards him, shoving against his thumb.

"You what?" *You liked it, didn't you, honey. Oh, yeah, you liked it.*

"I loved it. Wanted more."

She was a spitfire and no mistake. He narrowed his eyes until they were almost closed and breathed deeply. A fresh waft of her cunt washed over him, so strong he'd swear he could taste it. He eased the pressure off her clit, to tease, to make her needy.

"You want me to smack your ass again?" he asked, ghosting featherlight rotations on her clit.

"Yes."

"Your bare, sexy-as-sin ass?"

"Yes."

He could take no more. He stopped touching her and lowered his hand, finally able to look at her face. Her cheeks, flushed a vivid pink, deepened to crimson as she stared into his eyes. The stain of arousal coated her upper chest, patches that he would always associate with her needing him now. In his peripheral he saw her chest heaving, those gorgeous tits rising and falling as she breathed deep and long. Her mouth trembled, and he leant forward to gift her with a soft kiss, a barely felt brush of lips on lips, then drew away, lifting his hand.

"Taste yourself," he said, running his damp thumb tip across her lower lip.

She opened her mouth, and he slipped his thumb inside, where she closed her lips and sucked, swirling her tongue around it. He closed his eyes, coaching himself not to groan, not to take his thumb out of her mouth and replace it with his cock. His need to dominate her this way had always been strong, to break down this woman's barriers so she became pliant and obeyed *him* for once, but something told him she wasn't the subservient kind. No, she liked to dominate too much herself, and he anticipated fireworks in the bedroom as well as out of it.

Her talented tongue was doing things to his insides no other woman had—he risked drowning in her if he allowed her to take the upper hand. And she could, if she tried hard enough and gained more confidence. Later… God, later down the line they'd have such hot, sweaty sex, he knew it.

"Bedroom," he said, the word a growl.

She released his thumb and stared at him in shock, lips slightly parted, straightening her shoulders, a spark of her usual self clearly igniting inside her. *That's* what he'd wanted, her everyday stubbornness now, where she'd dash out a few orders and expect him to comply.

"Got to you, have I?" he asked.

"My God, yes, you've got to me."

She took his hand and guided him to the bedroom, letting him go to climb on the bed on her hands and knees.

"You want me to tell you what I want?" she asked, glaring over her shoulder, damp hair spread across her back. "Then smack me!"

Her sudden change turned him the hell on, pushed him to stride over to the bed and settle behind her, snug between her open legs.

"You want smacking, honey?"

She continued to stare, and if it wasn't for the slight flicker of her eyelashes he'd say she'd done this before. But she hadn't, was only indignant that he'd ordered her to the bedroom. If that's what it would take to make her true self come out when they fucked, he'd order her about again.

"Spread your legs further."

She narrowed her eyes, pursed her lips, but, by God, she did as she'd been told. She spread them as wide as they would go, and he stared at her ass cleft, at her puckered rear hole and her larger, wetter entrance beneath. He could sink his cock into either one of them and find heaven.

He reached down and fondled her cunt, sliding two fingers inside. She clenched around him and gasped, and he looked at her, daring her to hold back on him. She didn't—seemed she couldn't—and pushed her ass back so his fingers went deeper.

"If I've got to you, tell me what you want," he said, his damn voice betraying him, reedy and coarse, letting her know *she* had got to *him*.

"Fuck me and slap me," she said, straightening her back as though courage had filled it and given her some backbone.

He took his fingers out and licked them, telling her in his own way that, even though she'd suddenly found her fighting spirit again, he was still in charge. She groaned, gyrated her hips, and he knew she wanted stimulation.

He was getting to her.

She was getting to him.

Withdrawing his fingers, he smoothed one hand over her rounded ass cheek, casting circles to pre-warm the skin. She moaned again and braced herself on the mattress with one hand, snaking the other between her legs. He held back a smile at her boldness, congratulating himself on pushing her to the point she was at now, where, if he wasn't going to give her what she wanted, she'd give it to herself, embarrassment be damned.

He stared into her eyes as she stared back, her glare one of defiance.

Then he slapped her ass.

She cried out in shock, widening her eyes and dropping her hand from her cunt.

"You want more?" he asked.

She blinked, as though deciding whether she could take another strike, and then a flash of desire whipped across her face.

Yeah, he'd got to her all right.

"Again," she said, jerking back.

Impatient little wench.

He drove two fingers into her cunt at the same time as slapping her. She jolted, cried out again and returned her fingers to her slit. He plunged his fingers in and out, watching her arm move back and forth with her efforts to bring herself off.

He wouldn't allow her to get that far by just her fingers.

Taking his cock in hand, he guided it to her cunt, drawing his fingers away from her. She hung her head, seeming to look down at her fretting fingers, and he positioned the tip of his dick ready to slide in.

"Do it," she said. "I'm… I'm already nearly there."

He pushed inside her slowly, her sheath unused to him, straining against his intrusion.

"Relax, honey," he said.

Her channel loosened and he thrust in to the hilt, her tightness bliss on his aching, throbbing cock. He gained a steady rhythm, her fingertips bumping his length every time he withdrew, making him speed up as an orgasm built inside him. He worked faster, matching her hand movements, and slapped her buttock again, his palm stinging from the harsher strike.

"More," she said. "Again!"

She panted, shoving back on him each time he pushed inside, and, Christ, his balls tightened so much they were painful. He struck her once more, the sound of it reverberating around the room. Her cry of triumph quickly followed by her cunt clamping tighter told him she was going to come. It brought his own orgasm crashing down on him, sweeping him away with a dick-wrenching, slit-widening expulsion of cum that flooded her channel. She screamed out her pleasure, jamming backwards and forwards to match his thrusts, and, fuck, he knew for sure then that he'd found his soul mate, the woman who was his ultimate equal in every way.

Another forceful jet of cum left him lightheaded, and he closed his eyes, neck cords straining, his ass jerking with a rhythm he couldn't control. He allowed pleasure to race through him and listened to Sarah's cries as they faded to deep moans then on to soft whimpers. He slowed, his cock tender, and stopped rocking. Out of breath, he roved his hands up and down her back, gliding over her hips then massaging her ass. She tensed, and he guessed her buttock was a little sore.

"God, that was good," she said, panting, lifting her head to stare at him over her shoulder again. "And don't think I didn't know exactly what you were up to."

He pulled out of her and lay by her side, holding out one arm so she snuggled next to him. "And what was I up to?"

"Goading me out of feeling vulnerable." She dragged a fingertip over his erect nipple.

"Vulnerable? You? Never." He smiled and kissed the top of her head, her damp hair sticking to his lips.

"Exactly. I mean, I never get vulnerable."

"Or embarrassed."

"No."

"Even when you've said something's embarrassing, you don't really mean it." He fought hard to keep from laughing.

She swatted his chest playfully. "No. And, just like you said, I'm stubborn and will always see things in black and white."

"Hmm. Maybe you want to think about that last one again."

She lay silently for a while, teasing his nipple, placing soft kisses to his chest every so often. Then, "Okay, yes. I'll admit it. I see *some* shades of grey, all right?"

"Only some?"

"Yes, only some, so don't push it, mister."

Epilogue

From the fence he'd crawled under as a wolf the night Clark had shot him, Travis stared out over the ranch. A bright spring sun bore down on him, warming his face and bare arms, giving his surroundings a comforting hazy glow. Everything looked tidier now, the grounds well maintained, the bordering fences fixed and repainted, the bushes pruned, their previously unruly leaves and branches shorn away. The house looked damn good, too, the inside renovated in the space of two months, the outside boasting a fresh coat of white paint. It could almost be a different building, what with the new tiles on the roof and a sturdy front door that had proved its worth over the winter just gone.

They'd worked hard and long to get this place to the standard it should be, replacing all the old furniture with new, Sarah finally clearing out her daddy's bedroom and converting it into an office. She'd learned to let go this past year or so, to see shades of colour, let alone grey, as she battled to accept that things couldn't be done as fast as she wanted or exactly how she'd envisaged.

She'd come a long way.

Come a long way in the bedroom, too.

Travis' cock stiffened as he thought of how she'd changed since that night when he'd first spanked her. God, he'd thought her a spitfire then, but she'd shown him she had more mettle than he'd imagined. *She'd* become the dominant one, ordering him around, telling him where she wanted his cock, his hands, his tongue.

And, Christ, he loved it.

Loved her.

He glanced down at his wedding ring, glinting from a slant of sunlight. Their trip to Vegas had been a blast, the wedding ceremony one hell of a touching affair that had brought a lump to his throat and the sting of tears. She'd made his life complete, and, apart from their usual ribald banter and small arguments, they got along just fine.

Life had settled into a nice pattern the last fortnight, all the building work complete and things going back to them just running the ranch. He still had a lot to tell her about himself, about the pack he'd left behind years ago after his parents had died and how he'd remained alone until meeting her, but they had years ahead of them for that. His wolf didn't faze her at all, and when he sloped off some nights to shift and run until his lungs hurt, she didn't question, didn't probe. It seemed she'd taken him, wolf and all.

He sighed with contentment and shoved off the fence, striding over the grass towards the empty paddock. The men had gone home an hour ago, tired out from a week of heavy work, looking forward to a restful night out at Macy Jo's. He winced at the thought of that sweet woman and shrugged off the heavy feeling he always got when he recalled that time. He couldn't change anything that had gone before but could sure as shit change the future, making it so his woman never went through anything so horrific again.

Reaching the house, he stood outside and gazed at it, double-checking that everything really had been addressed. Confident it had, he walked around the side and entered through the kitchen door, replaced from the one he'd fixed before with a mahogany barn door so that Sarah could keep the top part open when she worked about the room while still retaining her privacy with the bottom half shut.

She stood at the sink, hands submerged in dirty water. She turned as he strode towards her, smile transforming her already beautiful face into something even more stunning.

He loved her so much it hurt.

"Hey," he said, that one word incredibly hard to speak through the lump in his throat.

"Hey yourself," she said, taking her hands from the water along with a potato and peeler. She placed them on the drainer and dried her hands on a towel. "You satisfied?"

He nodded. "Everything's been done."

"Just like I said." She smiled then glared at him from lowered lashes, her stern look designed to make him see he'd worried for nothing.

"But I'm not satisfied." He rubbed his chin and stared at the floor, narrowing his eyes in thought.

"Oh, hell. What's wrong now? I thought I was the picky one? What have they done that isn't up to your standards?"

He looked up, walked over and stood before her, settling his hands on her waist. "They've done fine. I just said I wasn't satisfied." He raised his hands and cupped her breasts.

"Oh. *That* kind of satisfied."

"Yeah. That kind."

She went on tiptoe and kissed him, sliding her hands through his hair to cradle his head. His cock hardened and he kissed her back, pushing his erection against her lower belly.

She eased away. "Hey, watch it down there. Damn thing's so hard you could do some damage."

"I want you to do some damage," he said.

"Oh yeah?"

"Yeah. Bedroom."

About the Authors

Sam Crescent

Sam Crescent has always had a love of fiction, through her teen years she would find friendship between the pages rather than in an actual person. By the time she turned sixteen she discovered mills and boon and never looked back. She loved the quick happily-ever-after read. A guarantee that no matter what happened the heroes and heroines would always find their soul mate. After college and starting a degree, one lonely bored night she searched the internet looking for a new author to read. On that night and for the years to come she discovered romantica and erotic writing.

Natalie Dae

Natalie Dae is a multi-published author in three pen names writing several genres. She lives with her husband, children, and three cats in an English village. She writes full time and is also a cover artist and blog designer. In another life she was an editor. Her other pen names are Sarah Masters and Charley Oweson.

Both authors love to hear from readers. You can find their contact information, website details and author profile page at http://www.total-e-bound.com.

Total-E-Bound Publishing

www.ingramcontent.com/pod-product-compliance
Lightning Source LLC
Chambersburg PA
CBHW020425180626
46812CB00003B/1149

* 9 7 8 1 7 8 1 8 4 5 1 4 1 *